FOUR CORNERS VOICES

Stories · Poetry · Essays

FOUR CORNERS
VOICES
Stories · Poetry · Essays

Edited by:

Chuck Greaves · Lisa C. Taylor

Mark Stevens

Contents

Stories

Introduction

While the Four Corners region of the American Southwest is unique in many aspects, its diversity of people, places, and attitudes may well be its most notable attribute. Where else can you raft a wild river, explore a red-rock canyon, ski an alpine mountaintop, or climb among the ruins of an ancient civilization, all within an hour's drive of your home? Whether your interests lean toward symphony or rodeo, off-roading or archeology, you're likely to find both opportunities for enjoyment and a tribe of kindred spirits with whom to share them here in the high-desert heart of the Colorado Plateau. And "home" for many of us blessed to live in this special place is just as likely to be a hogan or a condo as a farm or a cattle ranch. It's not surprising, therefore, that diverse and compelling stories lie scattered and buried here like so many ancient pottery sherds, just waiting to be discovered, admired, and now, with this anthology, preserved for posterity.

Four Corners Writers began in 2017 as an informal gathering of local authors meeting at the Cortez Public Library to compare notes on the craft and business of writing. As the gatherings expanded, both in size and in focus, the venue shifted first to the Mancos Public Library, and then to its current location at Cortez's ZU Gallery, where guest speakers, workshops, and panels are presented to the public, free of charge, on the third Wednesday evening of every month. Then in May of 2024, thanks to a generous grant from the LOR Foundation and 81321 Launch, Four Corners Writers formally incorporated, obtained its state and federal tax-exemptions, and began planning to publish its first collection of local writing, all consonant with its charitable mission of "identifying, developing, and promoting literary voices in the American Southwest."

A region-wide call to writers went out in the summer of 2024 seeking short stories, essays, and poetry. In September, the editors set about sifting through the avalanche of submissions, making challenging choices along the way. Writing talent abounds across the Four Corners.

You now hold the result of those efforts in your hand. *Four Corners Voices* is a diverse compendium of essays, stories, and poetry that reflects the beauty, captures the spirit, and embodies the essence of this unique and wonderful land of mountains and rivers, canyons and desert. All the writing that appears in this anthology is either set in the Four Corners region or else springs from the imaginations of Four Corners writers.

Please enjoy it, with our thanks.

The Editors:
Chuck Greaves (Fiction)
Lisa C. Taylor (Poetry)
Mark Stevens (Essays)

A Massive Manhunt and One Mysterious Telephone Call

Gail Binkly

On June 19, 1998, I was in the office of the Cortez newspaper when the phone on my desk rang. A man asked about the police shooting that had happened three weeks earlier.

It was not unusual for us reporters to receive that type of phone call. In the times prior to the internet, people often called newspapers seeking information about events both local and national. When I'd worked as a sports writer in Colorado Springs, those of us in the office on autumn Saturday afternoons had to field calls from people wanting us to read them every single college football score.

This man, at least, wanted information on one specific incident – the murder of Cortez Patrol Officer Dale Claxton on May 29. Three local men – Bob Mason, Jason McVean, and Alan Pilon – had been charged with the shootings, but had escaped into the wilderness west of Cortez.

Mason turned up dead near Bluff, Utah, six days after the Claxton murder. He had apparently killed himself.

But when the man on the other end of the phone called the Cortez newspaper (which at the time was published three times weekly and had two different names), the remaining two fugitives had not been found.

I was willing to provide him a synopsis of what I knew. Three of us in the newsroom had been covering the shootings and the ensuing manhunt – me, my husband David Long, and our fellow reporter Jim Mimiaga. The fugitive chase had consumed us; it was difficult to think about anything else.

Around 9:30 in the morning on May 29, 1998, a Cortez woman was headed to work, driving north on County Road 27 just south of Cortez. Near the McElmo Creek bridge, she noticed the pickup in front of her pulling over. Not sure what was happening, she pulled over too.

Then she heard loud popping sounds. "I couldn't figure out what in hell was happening," she told me in an interview much later. She asked that her name be kept secret. "I thought it was firecrackers. I didn't think too much at first until I saw the guy with the gun, shooting."

Officer Claxton had been tailing a water truck that had been reported stolen in La Plata County the previous day. The popular 45-year-old cop, who had been on the force only a few years, called for backup when the truck's driver pulled over voluntarily. Claxton stopped behind the truck but stayed in his vehicle.

A man – believed to have been McVean – got out of the water truck, strode up to Claxton's patrol car, and unleashed a barrage of bullets from a fully automatic rifle into the windshield, killing Claxton instantly. Just to make sure, the shooter then fired another burst into Claxton's body through the driver's-side window.

The woman I interviewed said there were two other men waiting inside the water truck. She saw them clearly and they saw her.

The only other eyewitness was the man driving the pickup. "He was 10, 20 feet from (the shooter)," she told me. "And the pickup was right in front of me."

Stunned and terrified, she waited to die. "People don't understand the fear you feel," she said. "It is just unreal."

But the shooter just got back in the truck. The trio – who throughout their rampage harmed no civilians, despite numerous opportunities – drove past the two eyewitnesses and continued south on Road 27. They headed west on Road H, then turned south onto a dead-end road curving upward to the county landfill. Near the top of the hill they found a contractor outside loading an old flatbed construction truck, and commandeered it. The arsenal they had with them was already packed in duffel bags, which they quickly loaded into the new truck.

Their decision to turn onto the dead-end road is one of the lingering mysteries of the episode. The men were apparently familiar with the area, having taken their stolen water truck along a route that bypassed the truck port of entry. But why would they head down the dead-end landfill road? Apparently, no one will ever know.

Law officers from both the Cortez Police Department and Montezuma County Sheriff's Office were by now pursuing the three men. Driving the flatbed, the trio headed away from the landfill, retracing their path. They shot two sheriff's officers who tried to stop them—Deputy Jason Bishop and Detective Todd Martin. Both men were gravely wounded but made full recoveries.

The fugitives, one standing in the back of the truck brandishing his rifle, passed stunned drivers who had pulled over for the law-enforcement vehicles. They then turned west onto Road G, leaving Cortez behind, and fled into McElmo Canyon toward Utah.

Until just a few years earlier, few drivers had used the McElmo Canyon route because the pavement ended at Sand Canyon, a popular hiking spot. From there on, the road was a stretch of tooth-shaking washboard. Had the road remained in that condition, the fugitives might not have gotten very far. But the road was now paved and the men were able to wrestle their purloined flatbed around the tight turns.

Hopelessly outgunned, having seen three of their own fall to the fugitives' bullets, the police dropped back. The scanner crackled with confused and errant reports – a man on foot running through fields south of Cortez, a fleeing car heading south.

As McVean, Pilon, and Mason raced toward Utah, then-Montezuma County Sheriff Sherman Kennell procured a Civil Air Patrol plane and tried to follow them from the air. For a time he had them in sight. However, the pilot became increasingly nervous when he heard about the crimes the three had committed and the arsenal they possessed. When Kennell urged him to fly lower, he balked, instead increasing altitude. Eventually they lost sight of the truck altogether.

Forty miles west of Cortez, at the headquarters of Hovenweep National Monument, manager Art Hutchinson got a call on his cell phone about the shootings. He thought the fugitives might be planning to turn off the McElmo road and head toward Hovenweep. If he could get there first and block the turn, he thought, they'd be forced to head on toward Utah, and police might be able to form a roadblock.

Hutchinson leaped into his National Park Service vehicle and sped toward the monument's entrance on Road 10. He passed a car full of tourists, who had been serenely enjoying the Ancestral Puebloan ruins, and told them not to leave the monument. Then he turned left onto Road 10, which was at the time unpaved, and rattled toward the intersection with Road G, the McElmo road.

Before he was even close, however, he spied a dust cloud coming fast from the other direction. Hutchinson swerved into the ditch as the vehicle passed; he heard the crackle of gunfire. Then the men were gone. Shakily he climbed out and examined his vehicle. There were two bullet holes in the hood, but nowhere else.

As Hutchinson called in his sighting, the fugitives were whirling the flatbed around the 180-degree curves of an even bumpier road that turns west off Road 10 and plunges into a broad valley.

The driver gunned the truck down that road about a half-mile, then turned onto a rutted dirt ribbon leading into Cross Canyon. The men pulled into the thick brush along a shallow creek and hid the flatbed in the bramble. They left behind hordes of ammo and weapons, but took plenty with them. Then they vanished on foot into the wilderness.

After that came the largest manhunt in Colorado history. For weeks, more than 500 law-enforcement officers and National Guard troops combed the torrid, rocky terrain along the Colorado-Utah border seeking McVean, Pilon, and Mason.

A surreal atmosphere descended on Cortez and the entire Four Corners region. Immediately following the shooting, area schools were locked down until it was determined that the fugitives had fled. For the first few hours, law officers stopped vehicles traveling on the highways, often making startled tourists get out of their seats while police checked to see that the fugitives weren't hiding in the RVs.

In addition to the law officers from different agencies pouring into the area, there were hordes of journalists from all over Colorado, the Four Corners, and major media outlets on both coasts. (One reporter from back East asked police whether the fugitives could survive by eating nuts and berries available in the desert, which made us locals laugh.) Helicopters chattered through the air, taking off and landing in Cortez, lending a war-zone feeling to the normally placid days of summer. The Cortez police gave press conferences twice a day.

Despite the massive effort – which included heat-detecting instruments (useless, since the blazing heat persisted all night), an armored personnel carrier (which soon stalled out), and dogs trained to sniff out humans both dead and alive – not a word was heard of any of the three until June 4.

That was the day that Mason was spotted by a social worker who was eating lunch by the San Juan River near Bluff, Utah, a small town about 30 miles west of the Colorado border. Mason fired a shot at the worker, who fled and called police. Deputy Kelly Bradford of the San Juan County Sheriff's Office arrived on the scene and was shot in the back and shoulder. Fortunately, he was not critically injured.

Law officers eventually found Mason's body in the brush lying next to three pipe bombs, an apparently self-inflicted bullet wound in his forehead. A Glock handgun (the suicide weapon) lay by his side, along with a .308-caliber rifle. His body was encased in a Kevlar vest. His legs were badly chafed from wading in the river.

Now centered in Utah, the media and police frenzy continued for another week, marked by other bizarre incidents:

• The town of Bluff was evacuated briefly as officers searched for the other two fugitives.

• Bounty hunters began arriving from around the country, claiming special skills would enable *them* to find the missing pair (and get the reward that was being offered).

• A young man from Telluride floated onto the river in a raft and was nabbed by police. He said he'd hoped to encounter the fugitives and talk them into surrendering.

• Then-San Juan County Sheriff Mike Lacy sought to use aerial fire bombs to burn the brush away from the river, but the Forest Service would not give him permission in the height of wildfire season.

After I'd recounted a shortened version of all this to my caller, I asked him how he'd missed out on the news. He said he was calling from Grand Junction and couldn't get our paper.

I said the two fugitives seemed to have vanished at this point, and he said, "Well, there'll be big news in two or three weeks. I think they're going to catch them."

He said sometimes he had glimpses of the future, and told me what he believed: The fugitives were staying near the San Juan River, under stress and not getting along. They were going to split up. There would be big news about them in two or three weeks. Almost as an after-thought, he said a child would be involved somehow.

Finally the man said farewell.

Days went by with no more word of the fugitives, and slowly life began returning to normal. We started covering other stories in the newspaper.

On June 29, however, the hunt resumed near Montezuma Creek, Utah, which sits about 12 miles east of Bluff. There had been a report that the two fugitives had been seen the night before, armed and camouflaged, coming out of the riverbed to examine a water truck.

The person who reported seeing them was a nine-year-old Diné (Navajo) girl. She told police she'd yelled at them and they had fled.

But despite the frenzy of the renewed search, no trace of Pilon or McVean could be found, and eventually the search came to a halt.

More than a year later, on Oct. 31, 1999, Pilon's remains were found by Navajo deer-hunters. He had taken refuge under a tree on Tin Cup Mesa near the Utah-Colorado border. He, too, had apparently shot himself. (There are some who believe one of his companions shot him.) He had run out of water, apparently after traveling only a couple of miles in the more-than-100-degree heat.

It was not until June 5, 2007, that McVean's remains were found. A cowboy spotted his armored vest sticking out of the sand along Cross Creek a few miles from the stolen flatbed. The cowboy also found McVean's backpack and a few of his bones in a hollowed-out orifice along the bank of the creek. He, too, appeared to have committed suicide. His wind-up calendar watch had stopped on the number 30, which could have been the day after the chase began on May 29.

But this wasn't exactly closure. Many questions persist. What did the three men have in mind originally? Why did they want a water truck? And why did they react with such lethal force upon being spotted in the stolen truck? A charge of vehicle theft would probably have gotten them only minor penalties.

Why did they carry such an arsenal?

What led them to feel so much rage at law enforcement? Some of their acquaintances said they were nice, likable guys. Pilon owed $1,500 in federal taxes, but how much rage would that trigger?

Why did they apparently all decide to shoot themselves instead of going out in a blaze of glory, killing as many officers as possible? Did they ultimately have pangs of conscience?

Cortez's longtime police chief, Roy Lane, who died in 2019 after being in that job for 39 years, told my husband in a 2007 interview, "I've thought so much about it and I have no idea what they were doing."

Popular theories included a plot to rob the nearby Ute Mountain Casino (rather unlikely, considering their getaway vehicle); a plot to blow up the Glen Canyon Dam in line with Edward Abbey's novel *The Monkey Wrench Gang*; and a plan to establish a survivalist compound deep in the desert. But that was all just speculation.

The episode has been the subject of books and television shows, but it remains a story that lacks an ending, a story still shrouded in mystery.

For me, one of the oddest elements will always be the phone call from the man in Grand Junction.

He told me there would be "big news" about the fugitives in two or three weeks, that maybe they would be captured, and a child would be involved somehow. Ten days later, there *was* big news, though it didn't involve their capture. And a child *was* involved.

Did the girl in fact see the fugitives? Not likely, because they were probably already dead.

But the general accuracy of even part of his prediction seems like a mighty strange coincidence. Who would come up with the idea of a young person being part of the news about the fugitives?

The answer to all these questions, along with the three men, apparently died in the desert.

Gail Binkly, a Colorado native, has lived in Cortez for more than 30 years. She is a career journalist and the author of one book of fiction. She and her husband, David Long, both worked for the Cortez Sentinel/Montezuma Valley Journal *at the time of the 1998 manhunt.*

You Will Never Leave This Place

Vincent L. K.

The smell of the house you grew up in will always linger,
though you will forget where it came from when it passes
you in the street.
The way the sunlight filtered through the trees where you'd play
will always leave dappled patterns on your aging skin,
places where you remain young and warm
and in the bliss of something simpler.

There will always be a rock in one shoe, and a penny in the other,
and you will pour milk with the same clumsy hands of your youth,
put your shoes on the wrong feet,
and get lost in your sweater.
Your friends will have children that look like the kids
you biked down the hill with,
did history projects with, kids you fought in the schoolyard.
There will always be a squeaking chain on the playground swing;

and you will always smell wet mulch and linger a little longer.

You can sit on the swing if you'd like,
there's nobody telling you to come home with the streetlights.

You will always remain in your childhood home.
The weight of the couch will always leave indentations
in the carpet no matter how many times it's replaced,.
The walls will always remember arguments
and crayon marks and the height chart,
no matter how many times they are painted over.

You will always sleep in your childhood bedroom,
no matter how many miles you are from it, or how many years.
Some version of you will climb into your parent's bed
after a nightmare; some version of your grandmother is still alive,
pulling frozen grapes from the freezer
and kissing your cheeks when you cry.
Some version of your mother is making cinnamon rolls
from scratch,
and some version of your sister, or brother, is still watching over
the edge
of the kitchen table, swiping patterns onto the floured surface.

You will always have drawings on the fridge,
and there is a version of you
who still believes in magic.
There will always be a plastic Halloween mask in the basement
and a baseball game on the radio.
The TV will be black and white, the M*A*S*H theme
and infomercials filling your mornings.
Cereal will have too much sugar or not enough and you'll be stuck

on the same level of Super Mario,
and have to blow on the Super Nintendo cartridge
at least once to get it working.

Try as you might, you will never leave this place;
some part of you will always linger
because you never forget
the smell of the house where you grew up.

Vincent L.K. is a queer poet and artist based in southwestern Colorado, where they've lived for the last six years. They enjoy writing poetry, playing Dungeons and Dragons, drawing, and listening to music. Their poetry often explores themes of their experiences with queerness, mental health, and life in general, and they have read at numerous open mics held in Durango and they have read at the Durango Arts Center as a member of the "Red String Poets."

Death Without Taxes

David Feela

Outside the city limits a sign advertised, Gravestones: No City Taxes! I'd driven past the sign for most of the summer, a curiosity welling up from within me. Then one morning I followed the arrows and arrived at a closed gate with a dirt track heading into an old farm property. A plaque beside the gate read, Gravestones Open 1-5. The lettering was painted to appear as if it had been chiseled into stone. Way too early, I had no choice but to turn around and head back into town.

Wind had blown all the dry leaves from the trees by the time I thought to revisit my summer whim. The same sign stood beside the county road, and though I must have driven past it a dozen times since summer, it might as well have been cloaked with invisibility. Yet there it stood, No City Taxes, mounted and displayed on steel posts. I followed the arrows once more and arrived at the gate, still closed. Gravestones Open 1-5. My watch read 1:15. I waited another five minutes before getting out of my car. Attached to the wooden rail with strips of duct tape, a handwritten sheet of paper read, Closed: Family Funeral.

I peered down the gravel track and could see nothing but a broken-down pickup with a rusted, welded hoist attached to its bed, parked in the weeds. The rest of the place remained out of sight, behind a bend in the driveway. From what I could see of the property, the place reeked of neglect, as if city taxes hadn't been the only commerce with the modern world the stone cutter had tried to avoid. I returned to my car and started the engine. Pent-up heat gushed out of the vents, taking the chill out of my bones, and I drove back home as slowly as I had come.

This story, like all unhappy endings, should be buried here, because I only met the carver of gravestones once. After all, my parents had already passed away, my siblings regularly called or wrote letters, and depression wasn't part of my character. That fiber of curiosity that had tugged at me gradually went slack. Besides, I suspected the stonecutter might have been the one who died the second time I parked my car at his closed gate.

Then my sister killed herself in California, shot herself with a gun she had purchased for protection. We all wondered, that impossible question, the one that can never be answered. She'd arranged all her affairs, left a note to help the family follow her financial trail, and donated most of her household furnishings to local thrift stores before she left the pattern of her despair on the redwood deck. She asked to be cremated, her ashes scattered in the ocean.

Grief consumes so much time. The hours settle like stone. The lives beneath them grow pale. Maybe it was years, I'm not sure, but one day I got in my car and headed out of town. The gate stood open. Stopping in a cloud of dust between the house and a small open building about the size of a two-stall horse shed, I could surmise that the stonecutting must take place there, perhaps only when the weather required it. An old, rusted tractor wheel lay flat on the ground with a chain, hook, and pulley hanging above it from the building's rafters. Bits of stone cobbled the dirt floor.

What surprised me as I scanned the property, overgrown with shrubs and trees, wildflowers and weeds, was that the grounds were littered with gravestones, some of them blank, some partially carved, cracked, smooth, though most of them monuments to a craftsman's artistry. There was no order or arrangement for viewing the stones like a buyer would expect in a showroom. It was a cemetery for no one, for everyone. Single gravestones were leaning against tree trunks, a few tipped over, or caught in the act of falling against each other like oversized dominos. The place reminded me of a quarry gone bust, as if the stones had sprouted like teeth directly from the ground. I counted at least fifty markers before I heard a voice behind me.

"You need help?"

"I'm sorry, I was just amazed by your work."

"Those? Don't worry, they're unoccupied. You need a gravestone?"

"Who doesn't?"

"I don't charge city taxes, so the money you save can go elsewhere."

"I saw that on the sign. How much?"

"It depends. I'd say a thousand will do."

All the time we talked, the stonecutter scrutinized me, his eyes never shifting from my face, despite his habit of punctuating every sentence by spitting tobacco. He had a full beard, carefully trimmed, salt and pepper hair, a straw hat. His arms and hands were large, finely sculpted muscles, flesh and bone. When he noticed me glancing at them, he curled his fingers and shoved them into his overall pockets.

"Yes, I'll want a stone."

"It takes considerable time. You won't have it tomorrow."

I reached for my wallet, pulled every bit of cash from it and thrust the bundle toward him. His hands stayed in his pockets.

"No need to pay until I'm finished and you're satisfied."

"I'll pay up front, take all of it. I'll mail the rest tomorrow, without the tax."

"You'll still need to choose a stone, color, style. It takes planning."

"You decide, all of it. That's what I'm paying for."

"I'll at least need an inscription. A name. Dates. No mistakes."

"Just a first name. Nothing else."

"Can you write it down so I spell it right?"

"It's for my sister, Patty. It ends in a *why*."

A month passed before the phone calls started and another month before they quit. I still drive past the sign, tempted to stop, but I never do.

David Feela's writing has appeared in hundreds of regional and national publications, including High Country News, Mountain Gazette, Small Farmer's Journal, Utne Reader, and The Denver Post. Published collections consist of three poetry volumes, a Colorado Book Award finalist collection of essays, and a massive chain of online links. He lives in Cortez, CO, and his website can be viewed at www.feelasophy.weebly.com.

Navajo Tacos

Robert Smith

As the sun rose on the reservation
          of sacred land, Navajo Nation,
          I give a wide smile upon the land
     as a happy, lucky man.
As I wake to the sound of an Indian tortilla slapped,

as hands tossed the tortilla and it landed in a pan,
as an elder spoke in Navajo,
turquoise jewelry hanging from an ear.
Me, as a kid, cannot understand but can surely hear.

A relative awakens,
speaking in Navajo, and I'm amused.
Even in my culture, I could not understand a clue.

As night peaks of dark after dawn,

I dream of sheep by my feet,
As I stand above my home on a high peak.
My grandma appears where I stand,
speaking in Navajo, and I understand.

Is this a dream?
I say in Navajo.
Grandma says, *No, Shit Yazhi* (little one).
It's time for me to say
you have caught up to me.

Robert Smith is thirteen years old. He is a member of the Navajo Nation and lives in Towaoc, CO. Things that he likes to do that make him happy are writing and listening to music. Robert used to live on the Navajo Reservation in Utah, and he says it is mostly deserted. He enjoys the beauty in the things he sees around him.

Covid Comes to Colorado

Gustav Hallin

I live in two worlds. Both are within the spectacular Four Corners Region, my home for the last twenty-four years. The first, the intrinsically beautiful physical world, where austere desert piñon and scrub oak groves flourish under the cobalt blue evening sky, an Arcadian tree skirt encircling the volcanic rock spires of the San Juan Mountains. The second, the windswept world of one's free mind here, breathing in, time and again, possibilities hovering nearby, in rarefied air.

Here, we try hard to welcome, with useful information and respect, our visitors traveling in from around the planet. We couldn't have the kind of coffee shops we have without them, I'm certain. One recent group of tourists, however, was not very nice.

The first COVID-19 entourage arrived in the United States on January 19, 2020,[1] the first documented Colorado case being a cousin virus that hitchhiked on a plane from Italy to Denver, landing February 29. As we later learned, many of his relations had arrived three months earlier without any reservations (double entendre intended).[2] How rude! In mid-March, COVID checked into our Southwest Colorado pulmonic accommodations, our first confirmed case.[3]

My colleagues and I convened an urgent meeting to speculate what might be required within our hospital to meet any and all community needs. Nursing directors, department heads, and administrators, we were abuzz even though we had nothing but partial data and rumors on which to base important decisions. The spectrum of speculation was not small, everything from this is "just another H1N1 freakout" to "the end of the world as we know it" were advanced as possibilities. Outstanding.

We prepared for the worst. We dusted off the personal protective devices that our nursing director had brilliantly acquired during a previously nasty influenza year. This gear included helmets with their own ventilation and high-end filters. On my initial attempt to suit up, burning red with uncertainty and complete cluelessness, I might have taken fifteen minutes, or maybe fifty. Our maintenance crew executed plans to remake some of our regular medical rooms into nice and tight negative-flow isolation space station-type rooms. A new look for sure.

I naively thought I was ready for whatever was coming. I'd been trained in Chicago during the late 80s peak of HIV complications and hospitalizations. I'd been a fellow in Albuquerque during the thunderbolt strike of Hantavirus Pulmonary Syndrome in '93. And I had joined an ICU team in 2000 that was way ahead of the game, with exceptional teamwork and inter-personnel trust at incredibly high levels. I thought all that experience would come to bear on this new challenge.

Like many others, I underestimated the severity and duration of the pandemic about to hit us. The physical world we knew was about to implode, and COVID had already received some advance assistance.

This particular antagonist was a more abstract, ideological pathogen, the private equity mentality of prioritizing profit and share-holder value over everything else. This mentality was ushered forth by the business majors who promoted a sales and marketing philosophy that infiltrated even non-profit hospitals like ours. In fact, we had been infected for years. Sometimes capitalist incentives are too high, encouraging less-than-ideal behavior. With executives' incentives to save millions in the short term, quarterly budgets and service cuts started taking precedence over sustained community benefits.

While the rest of the country's industries had already been in this descending state of duress and depression from this money-oriented infection of mind, we in medicine were blissfully ignorant of this money-grubbing virus, assuming that no one would weaponize the unwritten trust established between the American medical system and its patients. Right up until we were absorbed in the early 2000s, without a noticeable peep from the American Medical Association, we believed that the previous hundred years of quality healthcare, balancing the expertise of nurses and doctors fairly with reasonable finances, would last forever. We were naive, and we were swiftly swamped.

They took fiduciary control from our local Board of Trustees without informing the community or the hospital workers. Staffing was soon "adjusted," not for emergencies but for basic levels. In addition, "less essential" specialties were cut regardless of how many hundreds of miles their former patients would need to drive for substitutes. Inpatient departments were sold to national private equity-owned groups with no knowledge whatsoever of the challenges within a rural area such as ours. Time limits were mandated for clinic visits. Finally, we 24/7 intensivists were cut from four to three in 2018. Sticking to conventional business models—a cutting rather than improving services—for somebody's profit.

The cutbacks were made, our defenses weakened, and then

COVID-19 came to town. We must have looked soft in 2020, an easy adversary, but the virus hadn't yet met my nurses. In March, the battle began.

The spike proteins on our visitors' backs were like an Arizona cholla cactus ball, grapple hooks sticking into the protective cell lining of our lungs,[4] snagging the castle walls guarding the treasure trove of oxygen, thereby generating a massive inflammatory war. Too often that war got out of control and the castle walls were ripped up along with their accompanying blood vessels. Fluid saturated the lungs like two loaves of bread left out in a New Mexico monsoon, air pockets fill up, becoming useless. Not good.

Now you'll need more than the 21% oxygen in our atmosphere and more air pressure from a mask to keep blood oxygen levels normal and a few of those air sacs from collapsing. For two straight years our hospital had two or three patients on the regular medical wards in that precarious situation every night. When they plummeted, it was ventilator time, and usually around 2 a.m.

It takes about five people in the ICU to "prone" the patient in the most severe cases. One resolutely holds on to the life-saving breathing tube in the trachea, and the other four carefully turn the patient on his stomach so more of the lungs toward the spine can be opened up with the same amount of pressure. After a few months this became as routine as stealing free coffee from the nephrology clinic.

This pandemic was not a tale of two cities, but of two different years, the first without vaccines, the second with. That first year, without effective vaccines, the virus was indiscriminate and egalitarian, democratically threatening every citizen. But everyone in the community, by and large, was still rowing the same boat in the same direction, teamwork. The second year, including the tsunami that was the delta wave in late 2021, showcased how incredibly fast and effective the mRNA vaccines could work. That stretch also revealed how many people had lost their trust in our institutions and refused straightforward, life-saving recommendations. Everything in life, we discovered, can become a double-edged sword.

I voluntarily got the first of my dual vaccinations on December 16, 2020. My second was on January 6th, 2021.

Each of us is and has always been, simultaneously, an individual with rights and a member of society with responsibilities. But now we draw and take aim at a life-saving and grandparent-protective vaccine? I never saw that one coming. Dual vaccinations had instead become a duel. I *wish* it'd been a typo or something, we all would've been better off.

My initial response was fury, primarily at certain national politicians—those with medical training who knew better, choosing to put people's lives at risk in order to generate attention-getting spectacle and campaign donations. I'd always thought Mark Twain's comments about those in Congress was over the top. He said: "Suppose you were an idiot. And suppose you were a member of Congress. But I repeat myself." Suddenly, I got it.

I tried hard to understand those who protested the vaccine. Our minds were made for physical survival, not quantum mechanics, not objective truth, and not psychological well-being. Universal objectivity and mindfulness are simply not how we were designed to roll. In nearly all of our evolution, staying in the group meant staying alive. We hunted in groups. We farmed in groups. We built shelters in groups. Maintaining group cohesion meant everything for a species that was physically as vulnerable as any other. Individual humans were never apex predators; we worked together to survive.

In 2021 I learned that devout anti-vaxxer groups come in two persistent flavors—science nonbelievers and natural-only.

The more common were in science-skeptic spiritual groups, who chose to remain in good standing with their peers while risking their own lives and the lives of the people around them. No one wants to be the apostate, and I now believe we routinely underestimate how powerful this force can be.

Science is a method, nothing more, nothing less. It can, like every other mental tool, be performed well or poorly, including in a hospital (otherwise known as a temple of medical science). But our unparalleled ability to symbolize in a creative way can also be hijacked toward delusion by trusted sources, especially if they affirm our group identity, even while leading us away from solid adaptive behaviors.

The other set of anti-vaxxers, the smaller "natural treatments" crowd, believed that a healthy lifestyle and lots of vitamins and minerals with anti-oxidant properties could turn the death throes of COVID around even at a late stage with full blown Adult Respiratory Distress Syndrome. Or so they've been told by well-connected individuals, their leaders, often with a nutritional supplement or two to sell. I would attempt to inform them that we were beyond the preventative stages, when those strategies were absolutely appropriate, but we now needed a much more aggressive, curative tact while on life support. Massive doses of zinc and vitamin C were not going to get the job done.

And yes, just like every other treatment in medicine, vaccines carry risk, but medical judgments are always based on the risk/benefit ratio, not whether any risk exists at all, and this vaccine's ratio was astronomically benefit-positive.

Since those days, it's occurred to me that the human mind, too, is a product of the natural world, and thus, maybe the creative inventions of our minds are as well. We have the potential to be mindful, artistic, and gradually understand universal truths. Imagination and adaptation, turns out, may be parts of life, too.

In this era of social media and the prospect of information overload, of both accurate and completely inaccurate varieties, perhaps we should become more aware of a downside, the dark side, of our remarkably creative minds. Under the right circumstances we all can be convinced by identity-affirming visions inside our heads, rather than even the clearest evidence before our eyes. Choosing our heroes wisely is optional. Choosing our leaders wisely is existential. Leaders in government, in finance, on media, and even in non-profit hospital board rooms, can lead us astray.

Well into our second year of COVID, the sales and marketing department 340 miles away on the Front Range, twiddling in their air-conditioned C-suites, never bothered to show up on the actual medical floors for troop support. We didn't miss them—after all, when the cockpit crew in a 777 is fighting to keep the plane flying smooth through a bad storm, it's not like we call the sales department for advice, do we?

But while our communities were in a pandemic and nurses and docs were in the fight of our lives, some administrators didn't feel they could even trust the public to tell 'em what was happening. [5,6] So, being from Chicago with a stubborn anti-authoritarian disposition and hearing too many anecdotes of my colleagues coming out of locker rooms crying and despondent, I decided to do it. [7,8]

Successful hospitals, being the ultimate democracy of highly trained individuals, operate with numerous specialties that pool their talents and resources, wisely cooperating for the benefit of the public good. During COVID the MBAs resumed doing a perfectly adequate job keeping us well-supplied and paying the bills. The medical professional/administrative balance had been, temporarily and weirdly, restored by the physical variety of the virus.

A few positives were also obvious by then. The mRNA vaccines, developed by hundreds of scientists over the last decades, worked magnificently, and will likely enable us to quickly and effectively combat the next out-of-control viral pandemic.

By summer of 2022, the pandemic was slowing, but my amygdala, I have to admit, may never be the same. Too many shifts had started with me as the wisecracking Bill Murray character in *Ghost-*

busters, and ended as his wackadoodle greenskeeper character in *Caddyshack,* stalkin' the gopher.

I'll never forget the military MASH unit stress, but I'll also never forget the strength our teams showed, the nurses and medical assistants who came over from the operating rooms, the recovery rooms, the emergency room, the medical and surgical floors, to help us out in the augmented ICU when we were overflowing with patients on life support. I'll never forget the female patient who gave me a beautiful piece of Native American art but tragically died a week later. I'll never forget the millions of Americans who supported us throughout.

Ultimately, our nurses, docs, respiratory therapists, and support staff, engulfed within a catastrophe for two years, were the superstars and they each deserve a place in our local history of this event. With unceasing resilience, they did everything humanly possible to save every single patient, even if, in the end, that wasn't often possible.

I'll also never forget how the original sin of American healthcare—making it regionally competitive, as if a normal business, and not regionally cooperative even in rural areas like ours—was turned on its head in the Four Corners. Brothers and Sisters in our area, including the nations of the Diné, the Southern Ute, the Mountain Ute, the Jicarilla Apache, and us newcomers, as well as every regional hospital, we all strove together during COVID-19; it brought out the best in all of us more often than not.

We all share the same two worlds, the physical and the psychological, and we do better when we expand the team and reciprocate fairly with one another. As I now look out into the distance, I see the jagged peaks encircling one of the Four Sacred Mountains, my gaze dreamily drifts down over the mesas and through the foothills, glides over the untamed river below and comes to rest on the old Western Main Street constructed in this beautiful wilderness. I hope we can continue to build on this new foundation and be healthy and prosper in both worlds.

Gustav Hallin M.D. lives in Durango, Colorado, practiced Pulmonary Medicine, Critical Care Medicine, and Sleep Medicine, and is a former Medical Director of ICU at Mercy Hospital, Durango.

References

1. (2024) "COVID-19 timeline," *CDC MUSEUM.*
2. McCrimmon, K. (2020) "The First COVID-19 Case likely in Colorado long before March," *UC Health.*
3. (2020) "First COVID-19 Case Confirmed in SWCO," *Durango Local News,* March 24.
4. (2024) "Spike Protein/S Prot," *Sino Biological.*
5. Romeo, J. (2020) "Mercy says 'capacity' a moving target; staffing a growing concern, *Durango Herald,* December 8.
6. Romeo, J. (2020) "Elected officials grill Mercy over lack of transparency about COVID-19 pandemic," *Durango Herald,* December 17.
7. Hannon, A. (2022) "Mercy doctor says open, honest dialogue plays role in public health," *Durango Herald,* January 15.
8. Hannon, A. (2022) "Mercy ICU over capacity for several months, doctor says," *Durango Herald,* January 17.

The Desert's Time

Emily Manning

To love the desert
you must go close
and slow down.
Take the desert's time.

Probably you will need a little boy to show you how to go slow in
the desert.
And maybe he will need you too.
No boy can ever be given too much loving kindness.
That boy knows how
to fall in love with the desert.

He can stick his
whole face
down on top of a spring poppy,
looking eyeball to orange eyeball.

He can suck in the sweet, sweet,
creosote after the rain smell,
fill his entire lungs.

Sit down with him to study sparkly rocks.
Get close enough to see the sparkles in each rock.
Every rock sparkles.
Not one is the dull gray you see
when your eyes are too far away.

Run with him through those mountains,
fearless over the rocks,
brushing shoulders with the cholla.
Desert majesty can be exciting.
And the desert sun can make you feel full of life, warm,
free and fast and agile as you skirt the cactus.

And when you get bit on the ankle
by a prickly pear,
this is the moment when you should be so lucky
to have a little boy next to you.
He'll understand if you want to sit down in the sand and cry for a
few minutes
while you pick out the needles.
He'll wait.
He knows that falling in love
is painful.
When you are in love,
sit yourself down next to the boy.
Sit under a Palo Verde tree
when she has lost all complacency and fluffed out in yellow.
And the shade rolls out just for you
and that boy.

Watch the hawks, red tails fanned, glide over,
every ocotillo arm risen
in victory for you and that little boy and for me
and for every other soul
who took the desert's time
and learned to love her.

Emily Manning was born and raised in the foothills outside Denver, spent a number of years in Tucson and Phoenix, and now calls Durango home. Emily met her husband in engineering school and they raised two boys who are also engineers, so there is a lot of nerdy left-brain stuff going on in the family. To get away from logic and analyzing, she enjoys hiking, skiing, cycling, and poetry writing.

You Always Wanted a Garden

Caleb Stephens

You always wanted a garden. Nothing big, mind you, just a bed out back with enough room for some carrots and snow peas, and a stalk or two of corn. You talked about it all the time – how you spent your childhood elbow-to-elbow with your mother, digging in the soil of your youth. You wanted to do the same for our son, to teach him the simple joys of hard work and spending time with those you love. You imagined the look on his face as he bit into that first sun-warmed strawberry of the season, the way he'd smile.

It wasn't a big ask, your garden. I wanted it too, but life got in the way. A doctor appointment here, a flat tire there. A trip to the vet with the dog. Something always seemed more pressing. Eventually, it became our inside joke. I'd ask to go on a hunting trip with the guys or spend the weekend fly fishing, and you'd say, *Sure, just as soon as you finish that garden.* We'd share a laugh, and then you'd smirk and roll your eyes at the door. *Go on, get out of here.*

A week after Brandon turned six, I decided to surprise you. You'd be back from your jog any minute now, I told him. We'd need to hurry. He was so excited as we unloaded the supplies from the truck and covered them in the checkered tablecloth you brought on our picnics. I set a bottle of your favorite pinot on top, along with two wine glasses, and pictured how your eyebrows would rise when you returned from your run.

You never came home. Another jogger found you, collapsed beneath a stand of bur oak with your eyes wide open. An atrial septal defect, your doctor told me. A hole in your heart; one neither of us knew was there.

Your parents wanted to bury you, but I wouldn't let them. You'd made me promise as much, that night we spent in the Catskills staring at the stars. It was a beautiful thing to return to nature, you said. The cycle of life: Ashes to ashes. Dust to dust. All of that.

It took a year before I gathered the courage to move the pile of wood and mulch and heavy plastic sheeting to the backyard. It sat on the front lawn and burned a yellow square into the grass. The HOA wrote me letter after letter. *Move it, or we'll fine you. We'll lien your house.*

I couldn't. I fell apart every time I tried. Whenever I looked at it, all I could think about was you. About how I'd *failed* you. You were everything to me, and I put everything else first.

I started on your garden today. Brandon helped. You should have seen the way his eyes lit up when we finished the box, the way he bit his lower lip and tugged on his ear. He reminded me so much of you in that moment. It made me wonder if you were there, hidden somewhere inside of him, looking back with your mannerisms baked into the coils and strands of his DNA.

"It's just like Momma always wanted," he said. "Don't you think?"

"Uh-huh." I kept my gaze low as I raked the soil. I didn't want him to see my tears.

It's been a month, and nothing will grow. Even the tomato vines I brought home from the nursery are wilting. I checked the pH. I scattered the limestone and sulfur just like the blue-haired woman in the checkout line told me to, with a hand spreader carefully measured out in cups. I installed drip lines and a pole with a fake owl perched on top to make sure the rabbits weren't getting at the seeds. Nothing worked. It's like the earth is poisoned. Like it knows all of this is much too late.

I brought you with me this morning. I carried you to the garden along with an Adirondack and sat there, staring at all that empty brown soil. I held you in my lap, in the only urn I could find that seemed to suit you, a light blue cornflower ceramic stamped in doves. Something about the color reminded me of Miller Pond where I saw you that first time, sitting on the bench next to the water. When I asked what you were reading, you told me, but I didn't hear a word. I was lost in the way you tilted your head, in the way you smiled. I loved that smile – it was like you were giving me a little peek at the sun.

It's become a ritual, this thing. Just you and me, sitting in our chair beside your garden. I sip my coffee and we talk. Sometimes about the weather. Sometimes about other things, like the way I can't seem to function at work anymore or keep the house organized. How, these days, I drink more than I should. But mostly I talk about Brandon. He's broken without you here. There's no light left in his eyes. He seems older than six, and sadder by far; sadder than a child his age has any right to be. He needs you now more than ever, and all I have to give him is me.

It's not nearly enough.

We spread your ashes this evening. I hadn't planned to, it just happened. We were outside, you and me, watching the sunset when Brandon tugged on my sleeve.

"Can I hold Momma?"

"Sure, but be gentle," I told him.

He cradled you in his arms like a baby. He looked at you like he was holding his heart. I knew then that he would never heal with you here. He would never move on.

We poured you into the garden together, just the two of us, watched you mix with all that dark, rich earth.

"She'll love it here," Brandon whispered when we were done. "I just know she will."

And when he said it, I knew he was right.

"Daddy, quick, come look. Something's growing!"

Brandon said it the next morning, standing in the kitchen doorway with his cheeks puffing red. And something *was* growing, but not what I'd expected. No peppers budding green. No fruit taking shape. It was something . . . else. An elegant, olive-green vine twined around the pole, thick with bunches of creamy white blooms. It didn't make sense for something like that to grow overnight. It was too fully formed, too exquisite. I stared at it for hours. I swore I saw it move.

Over the next several days, you took shape. Your torso formed first, followed by a face of intricately woven stems. I watched in wonder as your ocean-colored eyes flowered beneath a mane of mandarin blossoms. Then came your cheekbones, perfectly delicate, your ears and jaw and neck. It left me breathless.

I slept outside. At times, it was hard to see you through my tears, but I could smell you. Taste you. Lavender and mint, and something close to honey. Your hands formed last, your fingers reaching for me, extending in a way that made me want to take them in mine. But I couldn't. I was afraid you'd fall apart at my touch.

Brandon took them instead.

He slipped past while I slept. I never heard a sound. When I woke, there wasn't much human left of him, only a few slivers of freckle-covered skin peeking out from among all the vines. His fingers were out and reaching toward me in a mirror of yours, his lips curved in a strawberry-bloom smile. He looked happy in a way I hadn't seen since the day you died. He looked at peace.

I sat there all day, in my chair, staring at the two of you, wondering if I had the strength to take your hand. What would happen? What would I become? You offered no answers save a look, your eyes as blue as the day you died, formed in petals, your mouth outlined in pale pink buds.

At dusk, I stood and stared out at the pastel sky, at the mountains beneath, glowing on the horizon in warm purple imprints. I'm not sure I'd ever seen a sight so stunning. And I never wanted to again, I decided, unless it was with you.

So, it was with a full heart that I reached out, and took your hand.

Caleb Stephens is an award-winning author and Cortez native writing from Denver, Colorado. His novels include The Girls in the Cabin, *a psychological thriller available through Joffe Books, and* Feeders, *a speculative horror thriller available through Timber Ghost Press. His short story* The Wallpaper Man *was adapted to film by Falconer Film & Media in 2022. This story first appeared in his 2022 collection* If Only a Heart. *You can join his mailing list and learn more at calebstephensauthor.com as well as follow him on Instagram @calebstephensauthor.*

I Like Reading Novels About Old Men

Peter Martori

I like reading novels about old men,
people without romance, absent adventure,
men who use tools, live beside meadows,
near rivers, who drink alone and talk out loud
to themselves.

I live with bugs, spiders in corners,
webs invisible, appearing in lamplight, mosquitos
hunting up my arms, crawly things, tiny lives
traversing my great Saharan floors.

Old men in novels review their lives,
studying poorly for final exams.
They smooth the steering wheels
of each car they have owned, recall the smell
of their father's tobacco, their mother wiping

her hands across an apron printed with
strawberries.

Out front, beneath the aspens
red-winged blackbirds invade the bird feeder,
a troop of five, acrobatic, crawling about
the wired mesh, pulling seed from a sparse
line along the base, moving up, allowing
another to feed.

In the desert, old men are written in thin verse,
cowboys or criminals; only dogs dream.
They are men of action, character, failure, danger.
They build railroads, rob banks, dominate, drive cattle.
They are sad drunks, tolerated, escorted home
by their daughters.

Here the heat slowly piles up, hour by hour, wool upon wool.
I watch a cat out the window, scratching in the grass.
It owns this neighborhood, respects no boundaries,
lays beneath cars in the summer, on warm hoods
in winter.

In the books I read, old men catalogue their regrets,
tease out forgiveness from half-dreams, dozing without
caution, wake smoldering, un-startled, pinching out
disaster.

They favor whiskey and wood over wine and iron, dusk over
daylight, a day's walk to nowhere and back.
I watch the cat, stoic and still on the edge of the sidewalk.
It strolls across the yard, quietly slips into the bushes,
while doves peck at fallen seed.

Peter Martori enjoys the poetry community in the Four Corners area, the open mics and workshops. Meeting a diverse group of poets has rekindled his desire to write and share how he sees the world with others. Peter was born in Chicago and spent most of his life in Phoenix. He is now retired and lives full time in Durango.

My Last Normal Day

Caroline Brown

I marked my 71st birthday in February 2020. Or, as my friend Carol called it, the 50th anniversary of my 21st birthday. My husband and I celebrated in Indian Creek scrambling over boulders to a cluster of extraordinary petroglyph panels. When we got back to our truck, we enjoyed birthday chocolate cupcakes under a perfect blue Utah sky.

On the drive back to our home in Dolores, I relished the serenity and afterglow of a day filled with fresh air and clear skies, with just enough soreness settling in my bones to let me know I had pushed my body outside of its comfort zone. A day well spent. And that was my last normal day.

The day after my birthday, I went to the Cortez Walmart. Several people were wearing masks, but the other customers, and probably me, stared at them. All I needed were paper towels and Clorox wipes. Standing at the end of the Paper and Cleaner aisle, I remember trying to process what I was seeing, or rather not seeing. I took a photograph of the empty shelving, thinking what an anomaly the bare shelves were. The photo has an eerie disconcerting feel to it.

We started hearing about a Corona Virus, which at first I honestly thought was an illness caused by beer. There was little information and too much misinformation. My husband's office closed. My volunteer positions were suspended. We learned a new word. Covid.

The Dolores Food Market put a sign on their door.

> *MASK REQUIRED FOR SERVICE*
> *DO NOT harass or threaten my employees.*
> *Do not pout. Do not whine. Do not argue.*
> *This isn't political; It is basic health and safety.*

Like everyone else, we canceled travel plans. We obsessively washed our hands. We cooked and read. We took walks and watched reruns of Law & Order. We wore masks in public.

Notices were posted by the Forest Service in the Boggy Draw area advising hikers and bicyclists to *Practice Social Distancing Outdoors, Too*. We complied. April was filled with hiking local trails by ourselves as we avoided friends, family, and strangers.

My husband suggested renting a small RV so we could go on overnight trips, but evidently everyone else and their dogs had the same idea. RV rentals were not available within 200 miles.

Three days after George Floyd was murdered in May 2020, I was driving home on Lebanon Road and feeling considerably disheartened. About 40 yards ahead of me, south of the Old Lebanon School, a small herd of deer were crossing the road. I slowed down. They all safely made it across the street and to the fence, but were startled by something and became uneasy and skittish.

I came to a complete stop. The adult deer began jumping the fence, but did so with no running start. They jumped from a standing position. All of their leaps were successful. The only deer who had not made the jump was a yearling buck. A bad feeling draped over my already gloomy disposition. I held my breath. The little guy was obviously nervous.

He jumped and almost made it, but his back foot caught on the barbed wire. He was hanging face down on the other side of the fence. I froze for a second, but then pulled my vehicle as far off the road as possible and made my way down the ditch. He was bleating like a lamb, dangling from the corner of the fence where the barbed wire was double strand.

Pulling on the twice-wrapped strands of wire was futile. I moved a few feet down the fence and yanked where there was only a single strand. The tight wire slightly loosened. I said to him, "Hey little Bucky, I'm going to try my best to get you out of this, but you're going to have to help me."

In spite of not knowing if his neck or leg were broken, I started tugging on the rusty wire.

Bucky pushed and twisted while I pulled on the fencing. After what seemed like a day and a half, he somehow got turned around and was facing me, but still entangled. His feet were not touching the ground, but at least he was no longer upside down. Bucky was now suspended upright, similar to a standing human. His tongue was hanging out and I could tell he was exhausted. I knew he might not last long enough for other drivers to stop and help us. I thought about George Floyd and wished someone could have helped him.

I remember taking a deep breath and telling Bucky we had to get him out right away. My arms and arthritic hands were getting weak. We were face to face, like dance partners, with the fence between us. Bucky looked me in the eye and seemed to summon whatever strength he had left. He put all four of his hooves on my chest and pushed. He may have been trying to kick me. Whatever his motivation, we both fell backwards. He was free from the barbed wire, but lying motionless on the ground. With a defeated sigh, I stood up and started walking back to my vehicle.

I heard the sound of a miracle. Bucky snorted as he tried to stand up. He stumbled a little but regained his balance and pounced away to the far side of the field where his family was waiting. No broken neck, no broken leg. My hands and arms were bleeding, but a smile flickered across my face for the first time in days.

Years ago I read somewhere, or someone told me, or perhaps I just made it up, that it's against the law in Texas to carry wire cutters in your back pocket. If the ambiguous information is accurate, I have often wondered if Texans can have wire cutters in their backpack or purse or lunch pail? Regardless of what the law may or may not be in the Lone Star State, it is irrelevant to me. I now keep wire cutters in both of our vehicles.

My husband went back to work in mid-June but his office was not open to the public. He spent his days on the phone and computer. Two more unfamiliar words were added to our vocabulary. Zoom and Webinar. I engaged in numerous virtual events including book clubs, board meetings, conferences, classes, Crow Canyon Webinars, parties and gal pal get-togethers.

July 2020 was brutally hot. In spite of the heat, nearby Canyons of the Ancients and Hovenweep, as well as other local public lands, filled up with visitors so we stayed close to home. Some of those visitors needed a reminder of what Leave No Trace means.

A close friend passed away from complications of Covid in August. He was estranged from his family and before he became so sick he couldn't communicate, he asked if I would spread his ashes. On a random Wednesday, a medium sized heavy package arrived from a mortuary via UPS. It was a tad unsettling to see the words HUMAN REMAINS stamped in large letters on the box. I put the unopened carton on a chair near the bookcases and it sat there for a couple of weeks. My friend had left a note stating I would know what to do with his ashes. Actually, I had no idea where to take him.

One day I finally put the box on the passenger seat of my old Expedition, buckled the seatbelt around it, and we took our last ride together. I turned south in Dove Creek and it wasn't very long until we were in a remote and rugged landscape, my friend's favorite environment. It was quiet and peaceful. I thought about another friend who lives in New York City. She said the sound of ambulance sirens never stopped during the first six months of Covid.

By September we gave up trying to rent a RV and decided to upgrade our camping gear instead. Most of the maddening crowds had left, so we were finally able to enjoy overnight trips in our new tent. On the 2020 Autumnal Equinox my husband and I commemorated our wedding anniversary beneath a brilliant full moon in Canyonlands.

We carved a jack-o-lantern in October and put a surgical mask on it. We mailed our ballots for the 2020 election and crossed our fingers. In November my husband's 72nd birthday was celebrated with a surprise Zoom party. He was indeed stunned to see a dozen of his friends and family on the computer screen. Thanksgiving dessert was shared with our daughter via Zoom. She was in Portland. We were in Dolores.

We put up a Christmas tree. We baked Christmas cookies, donned silly Christmas hats and tried very hard to be merry and bright. Christmas morning we 'Zoomed' with our daughter while opening our presents and stocking stuffers. We assured each other that being apart was only temporary and our lives would resume in a different kind of normal, someday.

Yet another new term was added to my expanding Covid vocabulary. Tele-Doc Appointment. I was a little uncertain exactly what that was. It turned out to be just another version of Zoom. I had the same primary care physician for over 25 years but my annual Medicare exam in 2020 was a first for both of us. With the aid of his very competent assistant, we had a virtual office visit.

He asked how I was holding up. I told him I was doing pretty well, that it felt like I'd been training most of my adult life for the isolation, anxiety, and depression from the Covid shutdown. Having been exposed to my sense of humor for years, he laughed, but there was a ring of truth to my answer and we both knew it. He had been helping me manage occasional, sometimes more than occasional, bouts of depression, anxiety and agoraphobia for about twenty years.

It was hard seeing other people deal with their own despondency and sadness. The loneliness and separation from family and friends was brutal. A heart-rending brief encounter epitomized the depth of isolation for me.

I frequently met friends at the picnic tables on the Escalante Trail near Canyons of the Ancients Visitor Center. We socialized, social distanced, and were relatively comfortable under the shade structures. Some days we'd see a handful of hikers, but the table we chose sat back several yards from the trail. We were never approached or affected by visitors.

One unforgettable day began at the picnic table with a friend sharing good news. After she left I stayed for a while, enjoying the view of Sleeping Ute. I must have been absorbed in an engaging daydream because I never saw the woman and her dog until they startled me out of my reverie. My first impression was she reminded me of those assignments from elementary school: "Circle what doesn't belong in this picture." There would be a page with an apple, an orange, a pear, and a toy train.

The woman standing in front of me was a toy train. She could have been in her 40's or 50's or 60's. I could not tell, but she definitely looked out of place. She was wearing polyester slacks and a flowery chiffon blouse. I swear my Aunt Mable had a blouse just like it in 1963. Her shoes were suitable for church or a ladies luncheon, but not a half mile hike to Escalante Pueblo. She had an old fashioned hairdo that looked perfect on her. Her choice of lipstick that day was bright red. She was holding the end of the tiniest pink leash I've ever seen and at the other end of the leash was a minuscule white dog with pink bows around her ears.

Before I could say anything, she asked if I would please pet Sugar. She said Sugar used to go to the dog park and had many friends, but now no one talks to them at the park and Sugar was so lonely. I came around the table and bent down to pet the mini-dog, hoping to high heaven I would not accidentally step on her, crushing her fragile body and ruining this lady's life.

The woman began telling me she lived in Kansas and was going crazy. Her church had started holding virtual services; her friends were staying home and one was in the hospital. There was no one to go to lunch with or talk to so she packed a suitcase, put Sugar in her car, and started driving. She tried to interact with people along the way, but hardly anyone would speak to her. Somehow she arrived that day in the parking lot at Canyons of the Ancients Visitor Center, started walking up the trail and there she was at my picnic table.

I was about to ask her if she had family in the area. I wanted to talk to and visit with this woman until we ran out of things to say, and then send Christmas cards to each other the rest of our lives. But instead, from deep inside of me, something so intense, so physically powerful, started rising up until it stuck in my throat. No matter how much I tried to stop it, my face uncontrollably contorted and I broke out crying, which quickly turned to sobbing. I wanted to make eye contact with the woman and tell her how sorry and embarrassed I was, but nothing came out of my mouth except choking sobs.

She looked at me with kindness and compassion, then turned around and faded from my view. I tried to follow her and Sugar down the trail, but my legs would not let me stand up. I said to myself, "and you thought you were handling the shutdown so well."

There was something about the woman and her dog that tore through my soul and shook me to my core. There was a sincere innocence or just plain goodness about her and she was having such a hard time. I was incapacitated by a crushing remorse like I had never known.

I had judged the woman because of her wardrobe choices. I had determined she was out of place on the Escalante Trail and didn't belong in my picture because of her hairstyle and shoes. The truth was she was lonely and only wanted to talk to someone.

I cried for a long time at the picnic table. I cried because of all the loneliness and isolation. I cried because of all of the pain, suffering and loss. I cried for all the deer caught in fences. I cried for all the George Floyds. I cried for my friend whose ashes were scattered on the Colorado/Utah border. I cried because I missed my daughter.

I have thought about the woman and Sugar many times since that day. I hope with all my heart they are well and happy and are living their best life now. I like to imagine she tells her friends over lunch, about an unhinged woman she encountered in 2020 on the Escalante Trail in southwest Colorado, near a small town called Dolores.

As 2020 morphed into 2021, I often pictured my last normal day; the day we spent at the petroglyph panels in Indian Creek on my 71st birthday. Before we learned about Covid, social distancing, Zoom meetings and webinars, before we had to wear masks and wash our hands so often, before the Walmart shelves were empty and businesses shut down, before the sound of ambulance sirens echoed through New York City non-stop for six months, before all the sorrow and grief, before all the death.

To this day I measure time in terms of Before Covid. There is no After Covid for me, just Before. We adjusted to our cliché new normal. Following our second Covid vaccine, we slowly began eating out, booking hotel rooms, and going back in the stores.

The prolonged bear hug my daughter and I shared during our long awaited reunion filled me with a renewed level of gratitude. I appreciate every lunch in a restaurant or gathering with friends and family. I remember how it feels to not be able to do those simple things. I think about Christmas 2020 and the conversation with our daughter, assuring each other that being apart was only temporary and our lives would resume in a different kind of normal, someday. Our someday had arrived.

Caroline Brown lives in Dolores, Colorado with her husband, dog, and cat. She is retired from a plethora of jobs she's had over the last 55 years.

Chaco Canyon

Tiffany Mapel

It's breezy in Nageezi, down a lonely dusty road. Ancient Great Houses anchored to the earth, resting under blankets of sand and sage. They count the millennia as the earth breathes up a dust devil.

Celestial compasses tuned to the passage of time; counting seasons—
sunrise, sunset, moonrise, moonset.
Globemallow and yucca bloom as they colonize the landscape. A Solstice spiral sundagger marks the middle of time, of the year, of everything.

The Ancient Ones are still there.

Do you feel the cool breath of wind entering the Great Kiva of Casa Rinconada?

Do you see the council fires on the North and South Mesas?

Can you hear and feel the rhythm of the drums?

Do you see the turkeys strutting around the courtyard, always underfoot?

Do you hear the echoing voices of the children on the cliff above Pueblo Bonito?

Can you smell the warm scent of cornmeal, simmering in clay pots over open fires?

Can you spot distant travelers walking on the Great Road to Chaco, coming to trade and rest?

Pottery shards mark their way, dust rising behind them.

Turkey vultures soar on thermals above.

The warm breeze slows as earth holds its breath.

Tiffany Mapel is an educator living in Durango, CO. The desert of the Colorado Plateau is her favorite place to explore. Her poetry is inspired by her wanderings.

Lay-by Lullabye

Katayoun Medhat

Toenails painted as pink as the gum she is chomping on, Larissa blows bubbles that inflate like tumors until they burst with a dull plop.

"Having fun?" he asks.

"Come on," Larissa implores the screen, extending the syllables: "Come on!"

"Coffee?" he asks.

Another bubble bursts. Gum hangs in pink strips from the tip of her nose. She pushes out her tongue, licks at the strings, and pulls them back into her mouth.

"Come on!" she cajoles. She does not look up. Feet pushed against the table's edge, she rocks back and forth. Her leg muscles play against her smooth, honey-tan skin.

He boils the kettle, spoons coffee into mugs, fills them with hot water and passes one to Gregory, who raises his head and says, "Thanks."

"Why do I feel so grateful when anyone thanks me?" he muses aloud.

"Because you are a sad old man," says Gregory, stirring sugar into his coffee. Slurping, he reaches for his phone.

He stands holding his cup in which undissolved tar-black lumps float in a mud-colored brew.

He sets the coffee down, walks to the window and bends over the herbs on the windowsill, inhaling the scent of mint, basil, and thyme.

"I bet these would work as anti-depressants," he says.

"What's wrong with Prozac?" asks his son.

Beyond the window, hills roll toward the mountains.

He empties his mug into the sink, gathers keys, wallet, glasses.

"Going out."

"Pizza," Gregory says into his mug.

"No olives! No peppers!" Larissa says to her screen.

It is one of those days that could be spring or fall. The breeze is cool and dry and carries with it the tang of sage and juniper.

The road leads past single-wide trailers, lopsided barns, and small-holdings with unkempt yards. The hills are brown and barren, and in the distance beckons the jagged mountain range.

After the cattle guard he takes a left turn, passing a sign warning that the road is not maintained during winter.

A herd of bony cattle forage among thorny shrubs.

The road dips and rises through dense shrubland dotted with gnarled and stunted trees and with boulders that look as if giants have hurled them in a fit.

Asphalt turns to gravel. There are no more dwellings, no fencing, no signs of human habitation. The road dips and rises, twists and turns, offering from any angle a desolation of shrubland and boulders and little else. The vehicle bounces and jolts over dusty washboard.

It is much farther than he remembers. Just as he contemplates turning back, there's the lay-by, a gravel-strewn patch.

Just as it was then.

He pulls over.

It's been years. Decades? It has been decades. And here it is, just as it was then.

He steps out of the car. All is silent; a heavy silence that makes him feel that he is moving within a giant bell jar. All may be as it was then, but he has difficulties picking out the boulder. Back then there was a footpath, he seems to remember. In any case, he cannot remember having to decide on a route to the boulder.

There it is. He's pretty certain this is it. It looks just as it did then.

It sits on an outcrop, a stretch of raised ground on the edge of an incline that makes it look like a watchtower, a lighthouse looming over a vast, arid expanse, this desert sea.

A meadowlark rises, loops briefly, dives back into the brush.

He steps over sagebrush and dried branches, kicks tumbleweed out of the way, stumbles over gnarled roots.

He cannot remember the walk from car to boulder the last time.

He can remember loop-earrings wobbling against pale freckled cheeks, a skirt riding up over white dimpled thighs, buck teeth worrying lower lip, eyebrows the color of sand. The way she pulls at the skirt's hem to cover her thighs.

Why did she get out of the car?

She didn't want to. That he remembers.

How she licks her dry lips and swallows. How her earrings wobble.

Why did she walk with him?

How she trips over roots and rocks on chunky white heels. How the cheap, too-short skirt rides up her legs.

How she is worried. How she is afraid.

As if all is a foregone conclusion.

What would she be now? A fat housewife with a mess of kids who may by now have spawned a few of their own. A grandmother with cellulite thighs and a wobbly lip. A doormat, there to be trampled upon.

He stands under the boulder.

The meek don't inherit the earth.

He stands on the ground under which she lies.

He doesn't feel much.

He doesn't feel anything.

Perhaps an idle curiosity as to whether she's been missed by anyone.

He looks at the ground beneath the boulder. It looks no different from all the ground around.

He had assumed that this patch would be more fertile, spur some growth. Maybe there have been flowers. Been and gone.

By now she is a bundle of bones, this fat housewife-to-be with dimpled knees.

He smooths the soil with the tip of his shoe.

"Hello there," he says. "It's me."

He pulls off lichen growing along a crack in the boulder, plucks it into small pieces and lets them drift to the ground.

"Just came to see how you are," he says and bends down, gathering the lichen and patting it into a little mound.

How still it is. How calm. How clear. How clean.

"I may drop by to see you again," he says.

He puts his hand on the boulder and pats it, prods the mound of lichen with the tip of his shoe.

The road to town leads east along the foothills. The peaks in the distance are shrouded in a wisp of clouds. They look as if someone has draped a lace shawl over them.

He makes it back home just in time for lunch.

He opens the door bearing three cardboard boxes.

"Pizza!" he calls. "Olives! Peppers!"

Katayoun Medhat is the author of The Milagro Mysteries, featuring unlikely cop Franz Kafka. She lives in the UK and likes to spend her summers in the Four Corners, where she is grateful, every day, for Cortez's wonderful outdoor pool. You can find her at www.katayounmedhat.com.

My Desert

Gennys Moulton

Behind the house where I grew up,
we built a fort out of dry sagebrush and fence posts,
scavenged old pots and pans from the neighbors
who packed up one day, and threw their whole lives away—
old couches, and a microwave,
a life that was ours for the taking.
A hole between two junipers
became a portal we could escape through
in our play-pretend. We were survivors,
we were loners, no parents, no tie-downs.
We fought giants on the mesa,
built fairy houses between prickly-pears and yucca.
One year I buried a time-capsule,
an old yogurt container we used as Tupperware.
I put in a picture of us, a newspaper headline, an old toy,
buried it beneath a baby juniper
halfway up the gas-line.

Deep-set tire tread was my stomping ground,
crawl up the side of the mesa, about halfway, remember?
We called that place Mars,
rolling hills of red, hard packed dirt, our New Mexico slip and slide.
In the winter we would sled over two inches of dirty snow,
rocks and cactus, screaming with pure joy.
I used to walk to your house on the highway, hair pulled tight in
a ponytail,
cross the old bridge over the Rio Grande,
creaking wood, whitewater beneath my feet.
I know that old ranch like I know desert heat,
smoked weed for the first time in a rusted, broken-down truck.
We threw rocks at old trailers, broken glass, old timers.
Girl Scouts in the mountains, scavenging herbs and flowers to
turn into tonic,
echinacea and osha root, lemon water and ginger,
hiking to higher climes, noses against the bark.
Doesn't it smell like vanilla?
Doesn't it smell like home?
I used to imagine the Rio Grande was an ocean,
hiking down cliff-side to touch the water, ant-filled beaches,
visiting cold white caves in Dixon.
God, the desert made me fearless.
No shoes, picking goat-heads out of dirt-tough feet,
coyotes howling past the whine of cars down by the highway,
driving through the canyon, so close to cliff's edge.
Whenever I see the gorge, I still catch my breath.
Drinking in the woods, pine needles beneath our toes,
music pumping out of my old Toyota Corolla.
We could see every star in the Milky Way.
I could hold my fingers above my head and feel immensity in space.

New Mexico, I can never leave you, not truly.
You are spread out beneath my skin like cactus roots,
the smell of sweet sagebrush on my fingertips after rain.

Gennys Moulton was born and raised in Northern New Mexico. They moved to Durango, Colorado in 2019 to pursue a writing degree at Fort Lewis College. Their writing has been published in Images Magazine, but mostly lives in notebooks, computer documents, and inside their own head.

The Search for Ian

B e t h   H e n s h a w

June 24, 2023
Night 1
11:00 PM
"911 what's your emergency?"

I gulped.

"Hi, I'm calling to report a missing hiker," I said, feeling like a ten year old that just accepted a dare to dial 911.

"Name, last known location?" the operator asked.

"Ian O'Brien. Last seen on top of Hesperus Mountain. 6'5" with blue eyes. We're camping up Echo Basin Road, at Lucy Halls Park," I said. My voice quivered in my mind, but came out steady as my Wilderness First Responder medical training kicked in.

"Lucy Halls Park, hmm where is that…okay, I found it. Alright, a sheriff will be out there soon," the operator said as casually as a fast food worker telling you to pull up to the second window.

"Okay," I said, ripping apart my lips which were stuck together like glue.

"I'll call search and rescue, but it'll take them a bit longer to get up there," the operator added, sounding tired.

"Thank you," I said. "Um, should I…stay in cell phone service?"

"Yes, that would be helpful until the sheriff arrives. Is this a good phone number for you?"

I nodded, then forced myself to utter the words out loud. "Yes."

9:00 PM: *Two hours earlier*

"Where's Ian?" Dan demanded.

"Oh, he'll be back soon," I said, eyes glued to the flames.

"But it's dark," Dan said.

"Eh, there's still some light left," I said, looking up and pointing to the horizon holding the last light, not yet full of stars. "He's got a headlamp. And he's used to running at night because it's so hot in Page. It doesn't go below 95 degrees until the sun sets."

"That's so hot," Mike said, shaking his head. Dan's eyes bore into mine, not yet soothed.

"Ian is training for a hundred mile race. He said he'd be back in seven hours," I shrugged. Being the partner of an extreme athlete like Ian required a lot of trust, freedom, and acceptance for the abnormal.

"When did he leave?" Dan asked, not yet able to sit and relax in his camp chair.

After checking my watch I said, "About six or seven hours ago."

Dan bit his lip and looked back and forth between me and the darkening forest.

Sighing, I pointed to a large log on the fire and said, "If he isn't back by the time that log burns, we'll panic."

10:00 PM: *One hour earlier*

"We should call Search and Rescue," Dan said, standing up before the large log turned to ash. Rachel nodded in agreement, her feather clip bobbing up and down in her purple hair. We all knew it was common for Ian to go out for an adventure and run more miles than he planned. Ian knew these mountains better than any of us. He could handle himself, unless…

"Beth," Rachel said softly. I looked at her across the fire and nodded. We were all thinking the same thing: what if Ian had a seizure and needed help? Epilepsy was the only thing he couldn't handle himself, especially if he got a head injury from falling.

"I don't have service here. I-I'm going to drive up the road and see if he sent a message," I said. After three years of supporting Ian's solo adventures, we agreed on a strict rule that it was okay for him to stay out late, as long as he sent a message at dark updating me on the plan. Ian left with my GPS and his phone fully charged. Surely it was me who was making the mistake, being out of service. He probably sent a message with his location telling me when he would be back. I just needed to drive to service to put everyone's worries to rest.

"Do you want someone to go with you?" Dan asked, his eyes wide and alert.

"Um…yeah, sure," I nodded, feeling far away. My mind began to track the mental map of the mountain and surrounding forest, wondering what trail Ian was most likely to pop out of. Mike and Ashley stood up, ready to go with me. I looked at them standing next to Mallow, who lifted her head and wagged her tail.

"Alright, yeah…let's go pick him up. He's probably on the road somewhere," I said, thinking Ian was still running his crazy ass, loving every second of it and totally unaware of our worries. A brick sunk in my stomach as I pictured Ian having a seizure on a trail somewhere, possibly falling down a scree field and breaking a leg, or going unconscious from hitting his head on a rock. If Ian had a seizure, he could be anywhere, postictal and confused. But he's probably still out running, having a blast.

The way to get service was to turn right and head down the mountain, but I turned left. *Calling the cops won't help. Shiny shoes know nothing about this terrain. Ian needs me to find him.*

"We'll probably get service at some point on this road," I said to Mike and Ashley as a plume of dust kicked up behind my van. The faint outline of Mount Hesperus loomed over us in the night sky before we were swallowed under the canopy of aspen and spruce.

"He went this way," I explained as I drove. "Earlier this afternoon I took Mallow for a walk, and when we turned down this forest service road, I started seeing his footprints everywhere. Yep, this is it," I threw on my left turn signal out of habit. No one was in the forest except for us.

Ian and I both wear Altra sneakers, which have a distinctive track. On the sole of the shoe in the center of the arch is the outline of a little bare foot with chevron arrows pointing toward circular toe marks. Anyone who wears Altra shoes would recognize it.

"I've never actually ridden inside your van. It rides great," Mike said from the backseat.

"So smooth," Ashley nodded from the front seat.

"Over all these washboards? Yeah!" Mike said looking out the window.

I smiled vaguely and said, "Gotta love Trish the Tank."

"Oh shit, can Trish go down this?" Mike said, poking his head up in between the two front seats like a dog. Two ruts deep enough to swallow my tires whole appeared on the dirt road at a steep incline down.

"Yeah," I said, never breaking speed. Lining up my tires with the raised part of the road, I lifted my foot off the brake and coasted downhill.

"Wow," Mike said, unable to hide his surprise at our van's capability. Trish didn't wobble once through those ruts.

"The road just dead-ends here though," I said, stopping at a locked forest service gate. Ashley hopped out of the front seat faster than I could put the car in park.

"There's a trail right here," Ashley said, pointing to a faint foot path that disappeared into the tall grass.

"Hmm," I nodded, looking at the trail that plunged downhill, deeper into the dark forest. Suddenly reverting to my seven year old self, I looked at the path and pictured monsters reaching out to grab my leg if I walked down there.

"Let's drive up the other road, see how far we can get. Maybe Ian made a loop," I said, checking my mental map of the interconnected forest roads. Ashely and I hopped back in faster than Mike could untangle himself from the pillows and blankets in the back of the van. Mallow looked out the window, alert.

Ashley pulled out her phone and zoomed in on the map as I shifted the van from park to drive. Gunning it back up the rutted hill, I turned left again, toward Mt. Hesperus. The forest service road was steep and Trish crawled up the hill, bouncing with every washboard and rocking side to side over the ruts.

"Trish has gone way further than I thought, wow," Mike said, then turned to Ashley. "Remember that time we got stuck on this road?"

"Oh my god," Ashley said, looking up from her phone map for the first time.

"That sucked so bad," Mike mumbled.

I ignored them and drove up the rocky hill, reading the road like water, picking the cleanest lines to glide through. Trish was by no means a four wheel drive van, but she was a Tank that could tackle most obstacles. When the ruts turned to swimming pools and the boulders turned to a scree field, I parked in the middle of the road. The three of us got out, leaving Mallow inside the van.

We trudged uphill, expecting to see Ian's headlamp bobbing up and down as he jogged toward us with that big goofy smile. Hoping he'd tell us a crazy tale of how he accidentally ran twenty miles and saw a bear giving birth. But every step I took felt like the wrong direction. The sound of my own labored breathing and the crunch of my foot against rock propelled me forward. I had to start somewhere.

Maybe we should turn back, and drive the roads down toward town. Maybe Ian did a big loop and was still running toward camp, but from the other direction. Maybe Ian is already back at camp, getting scolded by Dan and hugged by Rachel. Maybe Ian was running down this road and we'd see him in a few minutes.

Every step I took further uphill felt like a waste of time. I stopped in my tracks and looked at Mike and Ashley. We still hadn't found cell phone service.

"Maybe we should go back," I said, uneasy. As soon as the words left my lips I only wanted to hike further up the road. Nothing I decided seemed like the right choice. A panic was rising inside of my chest like an asthma attack that no inhaler could help.

"Yeah," Mike nodded. "Let's find service."

Taking a deep breath, I turned around. We barreled down the road back to the van. Mallow was sitting in the front seat and wagged her tail when I opened the door.

"Hey girl," I said, petting her head and nudging her into the back seat. I climbed in and reversed while Mike looked out the back window, shouting stop when my back tires got too close to the ditch behind us. Ashley giggled as I maneuvered a six point turn. Finally free, I kept my foot on the brakes as Trish angled downhill toward the loose boulders and ruts that wanted to swallow us whole. Ashley disappeared on her phone again, zooming in on the map, trying to discern which route Ian might have taken to get back to camp.

Suddenly Mike said, "I just got a message from Ian!"

Slamming on the brakes, I whipped my head around, expectant

and excited.

"He summited Hesperus, he's on the way down," Mike said, with his phone pressed up to his nose. My eyes lit up. *Ian made it to the summit! It must be less snowy up there than it looks from down in the valley.*

"What time did he send the message?" Ashley asked, skeptical.

"Six," Mike said.

"Almost five hours ago," Ashley said, and my lips tightened.

"He should be back now," I nodded and put the car into drive again. I couldn't remember if he left around 2:00pm or 3:00pm. Either way, five hours down from the summit was too long if he made it up there in three or four hours. While dodging boulders on the road, I cursed myself for not listening more when Ian left, for not knowing his exact route or plan. *Or was it Ian who didn't have a route in mind? He rattled off ideas but I don't remember what he picked.*

When the washboards turned from waves to ripples, I lifted my foot off the brake and we picked up speed toward camp. Seeing our headlights, Dan ran out into the road waving his arms, wanting an update. We had already been gone for longer than we agreed.

"We're going up to service to call search and rescue," I said out the window, slowing down just enough so that he could hear us over the engine. Dan nodded and I drove another mile down the road. Parking as soon as we had one bar of service, I took a deep breath and dialed 911.

Ian is not the first person to disappear without a trace in the La Plata mountains. In October 2022, a runner named David Lundle went missing, and in August 2021, Daniel Lamthach. All without a trace.

When the search for Ian ended after sixteen days without finding a clue of his whereabouts, people began to ask: could this be foul play? Should this be investigated as a criminal case? What if he was murdered, trafficked, or abducted by aliens?

Modern society does everything in its power to convince us that we've conquered nature. That the wilderness is safe. That the outdoors is nothing but beautiful. With all of our roads, maps, cameras and documentaries, we want so badly to believe that we understand nature. We feel reassured that we have enough technology to beat the mystery of the mountains.

Our imagination can easily picture a human killing another human (thanks, TV), but we don't want to imagine the woods doing the same. We want our innocence. We don't want the wilderness to be truly wild. Because if it is untamable, then we have to accept that we might die out there and not be rescued.

My point being that I do believe it's still possible to disappear into the wilderness. Grateful even, for places that remain wild and inaccessible. Unmarked trails and an endless expanse of ecosystem is exactly what Ian loved most about this world. Unforgiving chaos and unique order in the seasons is what drew Ian's curious nature into the wild.

My hope is that we still turn to the mountain's mysteries for guidance. That we don't let this search harden our hearts to the wonders of the wilderness.

Beth Henshaw is a southwest writer based in Page, Arizona. She is an M.F.A. student pursuing a degree in creative writing through Western Colorado University. This piece is an excerpt from chapter one in her first book titled, The Search for Ian, *which she is currently working on and pursuing publication. You can follow her work on Instagram (blog_by_ beth) and on her website: www.empathicadventurers.com*

Procyon Lotor

from Latin meaning: "The Washer"

Dai Salwen

Rock radiates cool white in the glow of the moon. The world is silent except for rushing water tumbling moonlight into darkness. An occasional chirp or screech reveals the presence of others in the darkness. They pad across land and rest in juniper branches through these long hours. Noises amplify where eyes falter. Smells deepen as colors become a distant memory. Saguaros stand sentry on this land. Then the water starts gurgling a slightly different tune. A dark figure hunches in the rock-bottom shallows. They walk: left foot placed gingerly by right hand, right foot by left hand. Two-by-two they skirt the slickrock bank. They stop, turn, dip their hands into the moon's reflection, and roll one palm over the other, placing fingers into the depths, then repeating. They obscure what is in their hands, but the water whispers hidden secrets as they press their treasure back into the current. Eventually, they place hands to mouth, pause, turn away, and drift back into darkness.

The midday desert sun bleaches everything it touches hot white.
A canyon wren chirps. Kinglets twittle. I crouch on the slickrock.
Little handprints disrupt settled particles on the riverbed's smooth
stone. Two-by-two the prints travel. I place my hand, fingers
spread, above the water's surface as if to stretch my body's know-
ing into the story of the solitary raccoon who walked this land the
night before.

*Dai Salwen is an artist, a writer, and a guide. They call Mancos home
though they often find themselves in the deserts of Arizona, Utah, and New
Mexico. The title of this poem comes from the Verde River Valley in Arizona
outside of Cottonwood.*

The Cast Iron Miracle

Kevin T. Jones

Rex Jex was a well-known tough guy. He sometimes worked for the government, sometimes for the railroads, sometimes for cattle barons, and sometimes as an independent troublemaker. He was known in the business as a persuader. A hired gun. A leg-breaker. He acquired his reputation while still in his twenties, when, having left his family behind in the south, he came upon a robbery in progress outside a bar in Kansas City. He calmly walked up to the armed robber, looked him in the eye, and shot him through the heart with a pistol he had concealed under his long coat. His coolness impressed the victim, who turned out to be Clarice Gapp, a cattle rancher who had just sold 3,000 steers and was holding a large amount of cash.

Gapp hired Jex on the spot to serve as his bodyguard. Jex proved to be a natural in the security business, and quickly expanded his responsibilities to include debt collection, intimidation, contract negotiation, government relations, and risk management. With his expanded role, his fees increased, and Gapp loaned Jex and his services to some of his rancher friends in the Cheyenne area. Soon Jex's name was known and feared from the prairies of Kansas to the deserts of Nevada.

Rex Jex made good money in the contract extortion business and enjoyed spending it on the finer things in life, especially whiskey, fancy meals, and fine hotels. While spending a few days luxuriating at the Star Hotel in Reno, he made friends with the hotel manager, a beak-nosed, cross-eyed New Yorker named Clive Smythe. He and Smythe became fast friends, and he convinced Smythe to accompany him as his assistant, business manager, and traveling companion.

Jex spent his money as fast as he made it, probably owing to the recognition that any day might be his last. He and Smythe traveled throughout the west, and business was brisk. He managed to skirt the reach of the law, as he was careful to work in the shadows, to work quickly, and to leave witnesses, if alive, too frightened to testify against him. The closest he came to being caught was when he went to Meeker, Colorado, to convince a man named Wilkins to abandon his homestead and turn it over to one of Gapp's friends who was buying up farm and ranch lands in the area where an irrigation system was being planned. Jex was in a hurry, but could not find Wilkins. He therefore terrorized Wilkins' family for several hours before gunning down Wilkins' fourteen-year-old son Ray in front of his mother and siblings. When Wilkins returned, he reported the crime, but later changed his statement and said that his family had no idea who had killed the boy, out of fear that Jex would return and take vengeance on the rest of the family.

Jex and Smythe had come to Desolation Valley on several occasions, never saying much about why they were there and never causing trouble as far as the residents could tell. But a man with Jex's reputation brings an aura of suspicion wherever he goes, and when he showed up in the remote valley, everyone drew their breath, looked around, and wondered if he'd come to visit someone they knew.

Jex and Smythe stayed at the Desolation Valley Inn when they were in the area, and while they were always pleasant and paid their bills, and even tipped. Bill and Maggie Baggs, the proprietors, were uneasy in their presence and feared they would one day do something awful, like murder one of their friends. In addition, Jex's sullen arrogance made caring for him and serving him meals unpleasant. Still, they treated him as they did any customer, with respect and civility.

One September evening, Rex Jex and Clive Smythe were dining at the Desolation Valley Inn, having arrived unexpectedly and late in the afternoon, expecting accommodation. Fortunately for all, a room was available. At mealtime, Mrs. Baggs rang her triangle, signaling to all that supper was served, and she cheerfully set about seating and serving her guests. Across from Jex and Smythe sat Jesus and Tomas Samaniego, owners of the Cross Arrow Sheep Company, a relatively large lamb and wool operation headquartered higher up the valley. They were returning from Hesperus, having gone there to negotiate a grazing contract for summer pasture. Tickup, a Ute Indian neighbor and friend of Mr. and Mrs. Baggs and owner of the Tickup Cattle Company, sat at one end of the table.

As Maggie Baggs brought out the meal – vegetable soup, braised beef, boiled potatoes, fried summer squash, and cornbread – a couple of late-arriving guests entered the room. Isom Dart, a tall and handsome cowboy from Brown's Park, was a favorite of all the ladies and was rumored to have been the lover of Queen Ann Basset and Etta Place at the same time. He was first to step through the door, followed by his friend, the noted horseman Ned Huddleston. They were two of the very few black men in the territory. Other than Albert "Speck" Williams, who ran the Green River ferry, and the family of Green Flake, one of Brigham Young's employees, black men were uncommon in the territory. Ned closed the door behind them and hung his hat on the deer antler rack by the door.

"Well, good evening, Isom, Ned," smiled Mrs. Baggs. "You're just in time for supper."

Rex Jex looked up from blowing on his spoonful of steaming soup, and he stopped short. His eyes seemed to burn from beneath his downturned brow. The Samaniego brothers noticed this and shared a glance. Jex shifted in his chair, turned to Mrs. Baggs, and spoke in a quiet voice.

"Ma'am, it's bad enough eatin' with these Mexicans and Indians, but I ain't sharin' my table with no niggers."

The room fell silent. Tickup rose slowly to his feet. His and Isom Dart's eyes met. Huddleston remained by the door, unsure of how to respond or what to do next. Mr. Baggs stood in the kitchen by the stove and moved slowly toward the side door. Maggie Baggs did not hesitate as she continued serving her guests.

"Well, all right then," she said. She walked to Jex, served him a wedge of cornbread, the very last, from the cast iron skillet in which it had been baked.

"Thank you, Ma'am," Jex said, keeping his eye on Dart as he reached for the bowl of butter to slather on his steaming cornbread.

Mrs. Baggs stepped back, and with a deceptively quick backhand, slammed the bottom of the 10-inch cast iron frying pan flat into the back of Jex's head.

"God forgive me," she mouthed, to no one in particular.

For years afterward, when Bill Baggs told the story, he compared the sound of the skillet meeting Jex's skull to that of a watermelon dropped on a rock.

Jex had had no idea the blow was coming, and he slumped forward, stopping only when his forehead smashed the cornbread to crumbs on his plate.

Clive Smythe leapt to his feet, and the other men readied for trouble. Jesus Samaniego later related that he'd been sitting opposite Smythe and thought Smythe might pull his revolver and start shooting at Mrs. Baggs. He said that the only thing that came to his mind was to pick up the steaming bowl of vegetable soup and be ready to throw it at Smythe if needed.

"I would have thrown it at him. I would have," Jesus said.

Violence was averted, however, when Bill Baggs reached over his head to his gun rack, took down his shotgun, and held it at the ready until everyone settled down.

"Take him to his room, Mr. Smythe," Mrs. Baggs said. "Clean him up, and I'll be up shortly to tend to him."

They weren't sure how, exactly, to care for Rex Jex, so they just kept him quiet and clean. His head did not appear badly broken, just jarred and kind of soft, so they placed cool cloths on his forehead and warm compresses on his chest, and after a few days he began to show signs of life.

When he first began talking, it was clear that he was a changed man. He spoke of the beauty of the fall colors of the aspens and scrub oaks. He complimented Mother Baggs on the flavors of the broths and soups she served him, and on the outfits she wore, however simple and rustic. Despite suffering a significant and traumatic injury, Rex Jex, under the care of his faithful pal Clive Smythe, and especially with the remarkable attention of Mother Baggs, fully recovered.

But he was never quite the same. As Jex was being nursed back to health, Clive and others gradually became aware that a fundamental change was taking place. He no longer seemed consumed by advancement or compensation; he no longer appeared to be willing to do almost anything, no matter how horrific, to obtain money. Indeed, he seemed to be mostly interested in appearance and fashion. While being mostly complimentary, he was sometimes critical, wondering why Clive Smythe would wear his brown pants, for example, with his blue shirt.

"If you're going to wear the blue shirt with those pants, you ought to wear your red bandanna about your neck, to complete the color balance," he'd say.

Jex began scrutinizing the clothes people were wearing, and cataloging them, and commenting on their effect. He pleaded with Clive to take him to the train station in Animas City so he could see what people were wearing. He sketched outfits for men and women on every piece of paper he could find. He begged Mrs. Baggs to teach him to sew, and so she helped him with a few basic stitches and techniques.

Jex looked forward to Tuesdays, when Eleanora Poultice came to give the children piano lessons. Jex and Clive Smythe would listen with rapt attention to her playing. They tried to sing along with her when she sang popular tunes, but she politely asked them not to, and volunteered to give them piano and voice lessons each week when she finished with the Baggs kids. Her lessons became one of Jex's favorite pastimes, and he practiced his singing and piano playing diligently, to his great delight, although not always to the enjoyment of others in the home. Clive seemed to enjoy the music lessons as well, and he and Jex spent many hours at the piano, singing duets and having the time of their lives.

Clive knew that Jex had spoken with some men from Telluride about tracking down Flat Nose Curry, one of the Wild Bunch, but was unsure what Jex had promised or if money had been exchanged. He knew that Mother Baggs's hospitality would not run out any time soon, but he worried about finances, and especially about creditors.

Things began to look up when the Samaniego brothers again stayed at the Desolation Valley Inn, having just attended a woolgrowers meeting at the Brown Palace in Denver.

"Everybody's getting rich but us," Tomas complained. "These big companies buy our wool for almost nothing, then pay slave wages to people at a mill to make it into cloth, then make thousands of dollars selling a suit of clothes or pants for five dollars and even more. It stinks."

"Hmmmm," said Rex Jex. "That's not right. Your wool is wonderful, and you should be rewarded. We should start a business. We could make the clothing ourselves. My friend Reba in Paonia is a weaver. Maybe we can get her to make cloth from your wool. I can work on some clothing designs, and we can find some people in the community to sew the clothing. Mother Baggs is a fine seamstress. Clive and I can get in touch with some of our friends in the dry goods business to sell our wares, and, well, my holy heck, I can't see anything to stand in our way."

And so began the successful run of the Desolation Valley Woolen Mills, which provided pants and overcoats, skirts, business suits, scarves, blankets, mittens, and an endless variety of related items to the region for many years to come.

Jex's specialty, and the real key to his success, was his foray into costume design for theatre companies in the region. His designs had caught the eye of a couple of young actors, who wore his creations when going out on the town and to parties. The fashions proved popular within the acting and avant-garde community, and were eventually noticed by Mitt and Orrin Mudd, who were producing the operatic spectacle "Helga of the Meadows" at the Wright Opera House in Ouray.

Mitt and Orrin fell in love with Jex's innovative use of color and form, and so contracted with him for the design and production of the show's outfits.

"Helga" became the hit of western opera houses, and eventually made its way to the most highly respected theatres of New York and Europe. Rex Jex and Clive Smythe made such a name for themselves that they left behind the site of their miraculous transformation to be closer to the business and cultural centers that were critical to their enterprise.

Rex and Clive did, however, return regularly to Desolation Valley. They maintained business connections with the Samaniego brothers, whose wool remains among the best in the region, and they loved to visit with the Baggses, to stay at the Desolation Valley Inn, and best of all, to have a piece or two of their famous skillet cornbread.

Cast Iron Miracle Skillet Cornbread:

1 1/2 C white corn meal

1/4 C flour

1 1/2 t baking powder

1 t salt

1 T shortening or vegetable oil

1T butter

11/2 C buttermilk. Sweet milk will do if buttermilk is not available.

1 egg, beaten

Some people claim a tablespoon of mayonnaise added to the batter adds some magic to the recipe.

Bring oven to 425 degrees. Place 10" cast iron skillet in preheating oven. Combine dry ingredients. Add shortening or oil to preheating skillet. Swirl to coat skillet. Return skillet to oven.

Add milk and egg to dry ingredients. Stir to combine.

Add butter to hot skillet. When melted, stir melted butter and oil into batter. Add batter to skillet. Return skillet to oven and bake 20 to 25 minutes or so.

For variety, add cubed or grated cheese, chopped green onions, chopped chiles, or whatever sounds good to you to the batter. Serve with butter, and honey after dinner.

Do not hit anyone over the head with the skillet. Miracles are very rare, and generally only happen in books and stories about the olden days.

Kevin T. Jones is a recovering archaeologist and redoubtable writer who lives off-grid in southwestern Colorado.

the names in our throats

Sarah Carr

Somewhere in the ecotone of no-longer-child and not-yet-man,
that waterlogged and treacherous ground, you wander
hood up head down
breaking in fury like a wave
against anyone rooted enough to take the weight

dear reckless, snare-caught boy,
I want to tell you how
to teach is to haunt:
we hover like ghosts, not real enough
in your world to move / matter
we listen, peripheral,
watch you simmer and burn

we are liminal,
a rustle of paper, shadow on a page,

begging you to follow us
down the tunnels we've found
between the lines

we dance and flutter
dim puppets behind a screen

while anger rises everywhere like a hemmed-in sea

and soft boys flicker and vanish
their names excised from your mouth
like teeth

what grows now in those sunless silent cavities?

what hides there? did you reach
into that festering dark and find
the gun?

what we cannot say will destroy us.

I want to tell you: to teach
is to be haunted:

by the hurt we can't hold back from you
the hurt we too once had to learn to bear
that has grown on us, layer by layer,
stacked on our backs like empty rooms
since we were young and raw
like you

by every word that wasn't enough
to pierce the veil
and call you home

by the names that gather unsaid
chambered and thickening
in our throats
layer by layer, calcite
and travertine
roughening our voices
til we gutter and cough
like crows

know this: teaching
is haunting.

do you remember
when you were twelve &
I found words worse than hate
carved on your desk?
I tried to warn those boys
that their words carried fire, bloodsport, slaughter.

they wouldn't hear.
you wouldn't look up.

that afternoon I walked west
and saw in the motethick window
of the abandoned mill
your name, traced in the dust

DIE carved on either side

do you remember
dancing on the riverbank in liquid
autumnlight, reading Frost
and throwing stones?
those boys slept on your shoulders
on the bus ride home
stay gold whispered like a toothless prayer

when the hold was called
what if I had called you in?

lockout: if I could have summoned you
to this side of the slamming doors
turned desks to barricades, thrown books
from the shelves
scrawled *l o o k u p* in red ink
on the classroom walls
would that have thinned the veil enough
for you to hear me?

how many books make a raft?
a signal fire?

or was it already too late,
would we have stood helpless and alone
on either side of the screaming void
of a loaded gun?

to teach is to be haunted.

I want to feed you bloodroot and poetry
help you vomit out the hate and hurt
that grows in you, a black and beetling mass,
creeps over you like kudzu, making monster shapes
of a tired bent-limbed sapling, of a

dear
reckless
breaking boy.

I want to tell you:
this is not all there is.

this   is   not   all   there   is for   you.

this doesn't have to be the part
where you calcify, or grow limbless
and curl inward, choke on your tail.

this can be the part where you drop the gun.
burn the script.

I want to call   HOLD:
please, just keep
holding
on:

there is no such thing as too late. &
this world is hard,
but it's also vast and wild and tender

& perhaps you'll never hear us,
but we are here, right here, just beyond
the shadowed and smoking edge
of youth's myopia-
gnarled and scarred, firm-rooted, full grown,
we circle
with arms enough
                    to hold you.

Sarah Carr is an educator and word nerd with a BA in creative writing and an MA in comparative literature who found home in the deserts and mountains of the Four Corners in 2017. She has been teaching writing for sixteen years, and occasionally writes things herself. She lives in an old barn in Mancos with her dog Modus and piles of bikes and books, and teaches composition, literature, and outdoor education to high school students.

Reflections on a Thursday in February

William Morris

Sitting at my desk, I am fascinated by the view out the south window. The winter landscape is familiar and foreign at the same time.

Straw, brown, gray, black, and evergreen are the underwhelming colors of this season in southwest Colorado. Well beyond the winter solstice and I feel the lengthening days in my gut and see the slow, relentless return of the light. Up close to the tree branches, it's clear that the buds are already swelling toward their spring potential of unfurling leaves.

In my sixth decade I know that the opposite landscape, six months from now, will explode with vibrant greens of emerald, sage, tourmaline, and ocean mist. These colors are vivid only in my memory and eager anticipation. I trust that the earth will swing around the sun in its proper alignment as it does every year. Confident of its regularity I am yet surprised, mystified, and delighted by the return of each spring.

But not too fast. Not before I revel in the subtlety and quiet expressiveness of the muted colors of the Montezuma County winter. A white-crowned sparrow darts between the dried stalks of Russian sage just beyond the window, searching for seeds of breakfast. Our dog, Nutmeg, snoozes behind my chair, sometimes shifting into the patches of sunlight offered on the carpeted floor.

Any grass that graces our property is desiccated straw these days, more useful as bedding for the floors of prairie dog tunnels than savory snacks for neighboring mule deer. The deer prefer to bump their heads against the bird feeders to lick up the falling candy of millet and sunflower seeds. So too the ring-necked pheasant cock plays the dandy rooster, scratching and pecking at the leavings of the red-winged blackbirds and the starlings.

Precious little snow so far this season. Skiers and water managers shake their heads and cluck their cheeks, wondering if and when the snows will return to the high country. In the valleys small patches of white cling to only the shadiest recesses behind tree trunks and rock walls. These remnants contrast with the dominant browns and grays, serving only to remind me of what should be, what might be, in a more typical winter.

Climate change has thrown out the concept of normalcy. While science helps to explain these changes to human minds, I wonder how the ponderosa pines, the sagebrush, and the elk will cope in the years and decades ahead. The earth and its inhabitants are surely resilient, but I wonder if our grandparents would recognize the world we are offering to our grandchildren. The same could probably be said of every human generation, yet I am baffled by the speed and severity of the changes accumulating in our lifetimes.

Perhaps it's a good thing that my friend the white-crowned sparrow cannot conceive of global warming or the myriad human dilemmas that shadow my mind through nighttime awakenings. I worry about my health and my family, the nation and the world.

With advancing years comes a wisdom that is frank and bold, stripped of the naïve notion that my life is somehow special. I try to live mindfully and gratefully, while noticing in my face the countenance of our common egolessness and mortality. The mule deer and the pheasant don't worry about death, focusing instead on the next meal and the sudden approach of a predator to be avoided.

My humanity is still my hope and perhaps my salvation. It is because I can fathom the complicated elements of global warming and I can still be shocked by the disrespect, indecency, and violence of human beings against each other, that I can wait for the tender buds of compassion and love to spring forth. I can work for the realization of the world our grandparents dreamed of, the fruit of their saving and sacrifice. I can play the small part allotted to me to help bring about the earth-dream of the Bible, the Koran, the Buddhist dharma, and the wisdom of myriad mystic minds and hearts.

I am fascinated by the view out the window of my spirit. The worldscape is foreign and familiar at the same time.

It is far too easy to slide into the quicksand of anthropocentrism. That white-crowned sparrow reminds me that each of us is a creature and a creation with an intrinsic value, independent of the other. Because we are so well practiced at altering our environment beyond our biological role, though, humans have a unique responsibility for stewardship and protection.

Nutmeg stands up and nuzzles my leg for a scratch. I'm happy to oblige.

"What do you say, girl, is it time for a walk?"

William R. Morris, National Park Service Ranger turned United Methodist Pastor, has explored and shared some amazing wilderness parks: Denali, Grand Canyon, Everglades, and Mesa Verde. He's a lifelong traveler, interpreter of Creation, advocate of public lands, and avid hiker. Will, Jane, and their dog, Nutmeg, live just outside of Cortez.

Mushroom Matinee

Stephanie Moran

Renegade mushrooms, alone and misshapen
unlike their happy pop-up contretemps
inverted pansy shrooms dusted with dirt
saucer shaped
next to melting
Daliesque domes
Japanese rice hats
demurely slanting earthward
horsecrab shaped
occasionally starkly upturned
unexpected and disconcerting,
like a child lost in the forest.

This one looks like a large puzzle piece crafted for a toddler.
In truth, I'm only three myself in this forest
and I see under the log I perch upon

a sweep of upside-down white ones
and cream-laced mushrooms like
seashells searching for their ancient sea
upturned gills like baleen from watery cousins.

Here a cup of amber ale collapsed into art
unnaturally perfect round skins with gills lifting up
instruments of soil and water open for the next downpour
offerings for a thirsty doe or wayward owl.
Here a series of flat mushrooms folded
onto each other like a dunny pancake dipped in quarter tone,
others wavy-edged and curving quarter-sized, pansies drained of
color.

Every fungi nameless and utterly unknown
but for my eye
at this moment
so alive
in these meadows and mountain sides,
a heaven's gate of mushrooms.

Today the eye-knobs of the aspens fly into bird shapes
wings in the downward thrust
throosh of wings before powering upwards again.

Quakies want us to understand their part
not just admire their naked bark skin
the upthrust bowls of sometimes four five, six, even eight
trunks rounding up from the same center
rising high to make a meeting place for the birds and the wind and
sprites on autumnal jaunts

here along the trail
we trade stories of this day,
sights hidden
until we hike and pause and look.

Stephanie Moran lives in the Four Corners of her beloved Colorado. Poetry brought her the love of her life and it sees her through the best of times and the worst of times.

The Tar Pits

Susan Washburn

"Are you sure you want to do this?"

Her husband stopped the car and peered at her through his black-rimmed glasses. His eyes were small and distant behind the convex lenses. His hands gripped the motionless steering wheel as if it might slip from his grasp.

"Yes," Marcie replied. "If I don't go through with this, I might not believe it really happened." She slid forward on the leather seat and grasped the handle of the car door. It was surprisingly cold, and she noticed her palms were sweating.

"Well, I think it's stupid." Her husband shook his head, his lips set in a thin, disapproving line. "You're just punishing yourself."

Marcie pushed the door open and swung one leg outside.

"Wait a minute," he said, and leaned over the gearshift for an awkward embrace.

She held her breath and stiffened against his encircling arms. When he released her, she exhaled and extricated herself from the low bucket seat.

She closed the door firmly but gently. When he'd brought the car home from the dealer and taken her for an introductory ride, he'd reprimanded her for slamming the door. *This is a Porsche, for Chrissakes. You don't do that to a Porsche.*

Now he ducked to peer at her through the passenger window. "I'll pick you up at Sanborn's after I finish work. I'll be there by five. Don't keep me waiting,"

Marcie glanced back at him. His flat, expressionless gaze was disconcerting. She averted her eyes.

"Don't worry, I won't."

As she set out across the empty parking lot, the guttural rumble of the car faded into a mélange of street noises. She felt the space at her back expand. She forced herself to look ahead, at the familiar red-brick building set into an artificial oasis of palm trees. No windows. Like a mausoleum, she thought, but at least it will be cool inside.

The soft asphalt pulled at the soles of her espadrilles. She felt as if she were walking across a tar pit. Had the La Brea mammoths felt this subtle tug as they drank from their dark, deceptive pool? Were they terrified when their massive legs sunk into the viscous pitch that would soon embalm them?

As she approached the building the heat reflecting from its walls scorched her cheeks like an external fever. She passed a gleaming white door with a discreet brass plaque reading "No Admittance." She took note of it. A rear exit, good for a quick getaway.

She went around the corner of the building and came upon the entrance so unexpectedly that she almost stumbled over a protruding step. When she opened the door a cluster of brass donkey bells hanging from the knob jangled. The sound pierced her eardrums like a metal probe. A rush of faintly acetic cold air stung her nostrils, and she felt the chill of the tiled floor beneath the rope soles of her shoes.

She closed the door slowly to avoid setting the bells in motion again and crossed the room to a receptionist's alcove. A placard on the vacant desk indicated that major credit cards would be accepted.

I don't want to use a major credit card, she thought. I don't want to get a major bill next month to remind me of this.

A girl with pale hair and butterscotch skin appeared in a doorway beside the alcove. The girl's white uniform and matronly green cardigan didn't suit her. She looked as if she should be lying on a beach in a bright bikini with her girlfriends, listening to pop hits on a boom box.

The receptionist smiled. Her teeth were as flawless as her skin.

"You got here quick, didn't you? The doctor will be with you in a minute. I hope you don't mind waiting." The girl gestured toward a sturdy oak bench on the far side of the room.

Yes, I do mind waiting, Marcie thought, but there's not a damn thing I can do about it. She took her checkbook out of her shoulder bag.

"I'd like to pay in advance. Is a check okay?" She was surprised that the words emerged so clearly from her constricted throat.

"Of course," the receptionist replied, turning to the computer on her well-ordered desk. Marcie wondered if the girl had an equally well-ordered life; perhaps she lived with a boyfriend and they drank wine and laughed while they grilled steaks on the patio and afterward made enthusiastic love on an Ikea futon. How would it feel to be young and heedless and happy again?

"That will be one hundred twenty-five dollars for the x-rays and medication." The receptionist studied the computer screen for a moment, then lowered her voice. "The euthanasia is free."

How gracious, Marcie thought. The killing is on the house.

She wrote a check and carefully noted the amount, the date, and "Valley View Veterinary Hospital" in the register. She saw that her hands were trembling as she slipped her checkbook back into her purse.

As she retreated to the bench, she glanced at the door leading to the interior of the building. She knew what was back there: white tile, stainless steel, caged animals waiting for a familiar footstep. She had left the dog there four days earlier, pushing him into a cramped cell as his toenails scrabbled against the metal floor in futile resistance. Once the barred door was closed he sat quietly, his big black head forced into a posture of involuntary submission by the top of the cage. He looked up at her, his amber eyes bewildered.

"Don't worry," she had reassured him, stroking his sleek muzzle with as much of her hand as she could fit through the bars. "I'll be back to get you."

Marcie's throat tightened into a hard ache. I will not cry, she told herself. Not now. Not here. I will not make it worse for him by crying.

"Mrs. Lundquist?"

Startled, she looked up. The tall, bearded veterinarian stood in a side door that had escaped her notice. He smiled at her and his lips flashed pink and naked in a nest of wiry russet hair.

"We didn't expect you so soon. You must have left right after I called."

Marcie nodded mutely. She had insisted that her husband drive her to the clinic immediately when the veterinarian told her that the dog had not responded to the steroid injections, and that nothing more could be done.

Waiting to euthanize him would have driven her mad.

"You can come on back now," the vet continued, and Marcie's stomach contracted into a trembling knot. She stood up and followed him down a hall past fluorescent-lit rooms containing steel examining tables, glass-fronted cabinets filled with medicine bottles, cylinders of compressed gases. She focused on his white-coated back to keep her surroundings at bay. Words drifted into her ears.

"It's really quite painless and quick. We give them an overdose of the chemical we use as an anesthetic. They don't even know what hits them."

They came to the room of cages. Furry heads turned towards them as they entered; expectant eyes looked out from behind steel bars.

Marcie saw the dog at the end of the bottom tier of cages. She cupped her hand over her mouth to stop herself from crying out. This can't be happening, she thought. It just can't be happening.

The dog raised its head from its paws and looked blankly at them. Then he recognized her and his mouth stretched wide in a canine grin as he thumped his thick tail against the floor of the cage. She knelt and slipped her fingers through the bars. He licked them, then pushed his nose into the crack between the door and the side of the cage and whimpered.

"Hello, Bruno. How's my good dog?" Her voice seemed to be coming from somewhere outside her. "You're the best dog in the world."

The dog's tail thumped faster at the sound of her voice. No, no, no, Marcie protested silently. He thinks I've come to take him home, but I've come to kill him.

"I'll be back in a minute," the vet said, and disappeared into another room.

Marcie tried to caress the dog's muscular shoulders through the bars, but it was impossible. She unbolted the door, and the dog nosed it open. She caught his collar as he lunged forward. When his rear legs hit the floor they splayed under him and his hindquarters collapsed. With great effort he pulled himself into a low crouch, swaying unsteadily. He strained against his collar, his nose pointed at the door through which she had entered.

"No, Bruno. Stay!" she commanded. The words stabbed her larynx. Why should he stay? His instincts were right; this place was dangerous.

The dog whined softly. He looked up at her, then back at the door, ears cocked, eyes bright with anticipation. He wagged his tail again and took a faltering step forward, but again his emaciated hindquarters refused to obey. He stumbled and fell against her.

An iron band encircled her throat. Strangling, she tried to speak soothingly but all she could manage was a croaking whisper.

"You've been a perfect dog." She stroked his massive head. "A perfect dog. You're my own best boy, Bruno."

The vet reappeared carrying a large hypodermic syringe. The glass reservoir was filled with a clear pink liquid that reminded her of a shampoo she had once used. She wondered if this liquid also smelled like overripe strawberries. A black rubber tube with an attached metal clip dangled from the pocket of the vet's lab coat like a lethargic snake.

"We'll just do it in here. He's used to this room."

Marcie fingered the wavy hair on the back of the dog's neck. Dear God, she prayed. Don't let this be happening.

The dog looked up at the vet and began to tremble. She sat down on the concrete floor and pulled his warm body close.

The veterinarian squatted beside them and extracted the rubber tubing from his pocket. Marcie closed her eyes. She saw herself standing up, flinging open the door at the far end of the room, the door she had seen at the rear of the building, and running with the dog across the parking lot. But the dog could not run, and she could not carry him, and he would never run again, not even on the sandy beach where he had loved to frighten flocks of inattentive seagulls into sudden flight.

The vet took the dog's left foreleg in his hand and wrapped the black tubing around it.

"The tragic thing about these cases is that the animal is so alert and perfectly healthy except for the lesion that causes the paralysis," he said.

She heard herself reply that she had known that Labradors had short life spans when she'd gotten the dog as a puppy, and she was glad that he had lived nine good years. But that's not enough, she thought, not nearly enough. How can I go on without him?

The vet pulled the rubber tourniquet tight. The dog tensed and shrank from him. It was going to happen now. Marcie tried to calm the dog with caresses but when he struggled to stand, she had to restrain him and order him to stay.

Bruno, Bruno, she thought, what a Judas I am.

"Okay, Bruno, we're just going to give you a little shot," the vet said. The hypodermic needle materialized in his hand. He sank the needle into the dog's leg below the encircling tubing and released the tourniquet with a quick tug. He depressed the plunger slowly and precisely. Marcie watched the pink liquid drain from the glass reservoir; she imagined it flowing through the hollow needle into the vein, traveling up through the foreleg to the chest, rising towards the heart like a cold and deadly tide.

The dog tried to twitch his leg away from the needle and she hugged him to her, crooning, "Good boy, Bruno, good boy," but her hands itched to yank the hypodermic from his leg and fling it to the floor, shattering the glass and releasing its deadly contents into a harmless pink puddle.

Without warning the big dog slumped into her lap. He raised his head feebly before it dropped as if severed by a guillotine.

"It's hit him now." The vet pulled the silver needle out of the dog's limp leg. "His conscious functions will be gone in a few seconds and then his respiration will fade."

The dog was an unstrung marionette. She leaned close over him and looked into his open eyes. They were motionless, unblinking, unfocused. His muzzle quivered gently as air passed in and out of his nostrils.

"It's all right, Bruno," she whispered, nuzzling his velvety ear.

She cradled his warm, solid neck in her hands, transfusing life into him. "It's all right," she repeated helplessly.

The dog's abdomen rose and fell erratically, then stopped. Desperate, she looked into his glazed eyes for some sign of awareness.

"I'm sure he's completely out now," the vet said.

Marcie pressed her lips to the smooth crown of the dog's head. Go in peace, she thought. I release you. Go from whence you came. The archaic phrase sprang into her mind of its own accord, and a shiver rippled down her spine.

The vet moved to the dog's side and applied a stethoscope to his chest just under the foreleg. Marcie could feel the cold smooth disc as if it were in her own armpit. The vet listened briefly, then removed the stethoscope and rocked back on his heels.

"There's no heartbeat," he announced.

Suddenly the dog's rib cage expanded and air fluttered out through his slack lips. Marcie gasped. Something had gone wrong; he was alive and struggling for breath under the leaden weight of the anesthetic.

"Those are just reflexive movements," the vet assured her. He stood up and pocketed his stethoscope. Marcie's heart slid back down from her throat.

She tried to draw the dog's eyelids over his unguarded pupils but the lashes were so short she couldn't grasp them. Holding his head up with one arm, she slid her knees out from under his body. She unsnapped his collar and gently lowered his heavy head to the floor.

She put the collar in her bag, stepped over the dog's body and walked blindly to the exit door. The veterinarian sprang in front of her to open it. A wave of shimmering heat engulfed her.

"I'm sorry. But this was for the best."

The veterinarian's words hung in the air outside her ears; his lab coat was a white blur in her peripheral vision.

She couldn't reply. Her throat was paralyzed, her eyes bathed in acid. She waved a hand behind her as she bolted into the parking lot and ran toward the street.

She jogged along the sidewalk, keeping her head bent so that the children leaving the elementary school across the street would not see the tears on her cheeks. She made it as far as a palm tree in a vacant lot before the hard knot of pain in her chest exploded into deep, wracking sobs.

At precisely five p.m. Marcie walked into Sanborn's Coffee Shop. She saw her husband in a booth near the bulbous, multicolored jukebox. He started to rise as she approached, but she shook her head and motioned for him to stay seated. She picked her way between the shiny laminate-topped tables and chrome-plated chairs and slid into the booth across from him.

"How did it go? Are you okay?"

His eyes bored into her skull. His hand on her wrist was a sprung trap. She stared at the embossed arabesques on the paper napkin lying in front of her.

"I'm fine," she said. Her voice was a hollow echo rising from a void. "It's over. It's all over."

Susan Washburn's publications include two nonfiction books, Partners *(Atheneum 1981) and* My Horse, My Self *(Casa de Snapdragone 2015), which won a New Mexico-Arizona Book Award. Her essays have appeared in The Broad Street Review, an online journal of the arts. Her new novel,* Gone Astray, *set in a fictionalized version of Durango, was just released by Cyberwit.net Publications and is available on Amazon. For more information, go to www.susanewashburn.com.*

Old Horse

H . C .   P e t l e y

Old horse is down
in the weathered corral,
his two horse companions standing by
patient in anticipation of his death.

We go by on machines
out to do potato rows
after two days of rain,
fog lying heavy on the fields.
Late in the day
fog comes in again
creeping up the shallow river.
We clatter in on machines
low on fuel, splattered with mud.
Old horse is up now,
slow walking around.

Now 83, H. C. Petley began his checkered writing career in 1960 at the University of Pittsburgh. His by-line has been posted in such disparate places as the Mainichi News, Tokyo, Astrophysics Newsletter, Melbourne, Galaxy Magazine, New York City, Los Angeles Free Press, Playboy's OUI Magazine, Chicago, and many others now out of print and forgotten. His picaresque comedy novel **Queen** of **Slots** *was selected by the Merchant Marine Library of NYC for distribution to all the ships at sea during the Gulf War. Rare copies can possibly be found at Amazon's Abe Books. Currently, he lives quietly in Cortez.*

Nahodishgish

Aidan Gaughran

Leaving behind the babble of the plaza, I enter the library. I feel, almost physically, the gravitation… the enveloping serenity of order, time magically desiccated and preserved.

—Jorge Luis Borges, A Leopoldo Lugones

There was not much to announce the trail—just a single-lane dirt road that gave way to a footpath, which after a short distance bled into slickrock. The slickrock boasted a smattering of cairns that made you wonder if they were cairns or miscellaneous jumbles: made in a rush or long ago or both, no more than a foot high. We zigged and zagged and after realizing it's all just rock anyways, we let our feet do the walking. At the edge of the slickrock, we saw what we came to see: the centuries-old skeleton of a rock dwelling, nestled across the canyon in a sunny alcove.

Below, a wash snaked around either side of the canyon, stretching out of sight. To arrive at the nook in question we would scurry down, cross the wash, and scamper up again. Spotting a half-cairn, we shimmied our way down off the slickrock and into sagebrush—the edge of the wash.

The sand was deep, ungroomed, cool. The sand seeped into our shoes as we made footsteps. Our wake resembled a trail of mini-craters, the sand falling over and devouring itself, grain by grain. Perhaps there was not much holding the ground together.

The wash measured more than 100 feet across; the water in the wash measured about six inches wide. Willows stood rooted in line on either side, eager for a drink. Up and down the wash, audible trickles came and went, taking turns between surfacing and diving down for refuge under the earth or odd patch of ice. It was a few degrees cooler down in the draw, a difference that tickled our feet and calves but did not extend past our knees.

We clambered on all fours up the cold fine sand, coming to the edge of a slot canyon that was home to a creature. We stopped and stooped our ears, listening in on the 100- yard-away thing as if it was just there, behind a closed door. Out of sight, the creature rummaged about on the canyon floor. It sounded like a child sorting through a leaf pile in search of a lost toy, muttering to herself in a muffled language only she could understand. She then let out a few shrieks that resembled a cat's MEOW but was most definitely a bird. Recognizing the call, I mimicked the bird. Skirting along the canyon floor, the bird revealed herself: a spotted towhee. She looked up at us from her juniper perch with that piercing red eye, continuing to mutter to herself, as if to say: you're not my mate. Not even a potential one.

The towhee parted, leaving us a short walk from the dwelling we had first seen at the canyon rim. There was not much to the nook: a waist-high rectangular room that led to a smaller chamber with an opening just large enough for a human to climb into. The entire rock monolith acted as the roof; from there it was mud, rock, mud, and rock all the way down. We could still see grass (and the tiny indentations where grass once was) in the solidified mud, along with a few additional support sticks poking out of the structure.

On the ground, there were small rocks arranged on big rocks. But upon further review, the small rocks became pottery shards. Some were clay, with a simple wave pattern, like hardened ripples of a creek bed. Others were more refined, with lines and diamond shapes the color of licorice. Then there were rocks that lay in stark contrast to the sandstone-scape: smooth and glossy maroons and blacks, with pointed ends.

I peeled off from my partner, continuing past another mud-rock room, running my hand along the sandstone monolith. Sandstone in the shade is alright. But when the sun hits sandstone in a certain light—well, the rock leaps to life. The minerals come out to play and envelop their beholder in a glistening lithic sea. Surrounded by sparkles, compelled by a gravity, I sat on a rock.

I took stock of the sounds I'd heard up to that point:

- the towhee, scratching and yammering in leafy sand
- the buzz of a fly (just one), in search of food and sun
- the gargle-gargle of a raven, passing by overhead
- the drone of a plane
- that tiny trickle in the wash, always fading

I realized that my partner and I had been speaking for a while at a whisper, as if in a museum, and that this came about unconsciously, because the setting had demanded it.

Looking down at the wash twisting in deep purples, yellows and oranges, I also realized the difficulty of seeing past the loudness of the mind, past its endless endeavors of registering and noticing "things,"[1] to be blank—truly blank. As if that wasn't enough, I had the sensation that someone, from this very spot, had watched me come up the wash. I tried to sit still.

---

[1] Robert M. Pirsig called this process the "knife:" "With a single stroke of analytic thought [Phædrus] split the whole world into parts of his own choosing, split the parts and split the fragments of the parts, finer and finer and finer until he had reduced it to what he wanted it to be."

§

The Anasazi lived in this area until (at the latest) 1300 A.D., long before conquistadores knew they were conquistadores, long before they first stirred in their mothers' wombs. Almost a thousand years have passed. It is quite easy to imagine this site, these pottery shards, going the way of Ozymandias—lost to the sands of time or to over-eager visitors. Of course, they are in the midst of that unfortunate process. And I am fortunately oblivious to it, to the wind that whisks, day by day, sand away from rock.

They exist. They are here now, and they allow the viewer to fill the vacancy with worlds of possibilities: in this room, we kept the corn. Here is where we kept the hides. Baskets to trade.

Wood for fires. We worshipped in this room; we laid our heads at night in that one. With full bellies, we painted bighorn sheep on this rock, to commemorate the hunt. Over there, we took sun baths on the sandstone before that flaming ball slipped behind the ridge. Here, we mulled over a forbidden love (remember?), laughed a bit, held a newborn up to our ears, marveled at its breath. We felt the quiet and dealt with the loudness, too.

It is tempting to chalk up the existence of this little piece of the world to tribal or federal protection—though there was not much in place to protect the place. No gate guarded the entrance (was there an entrance?). No glass box housed the relics. No sign gave explanations, filled guests' heads with facts.

Or maybe it is tempting to think of the place as some sort of arid Thoreauvian nature, or as a locale that housed an Abbey rant, its relative inaccessibility repelling crowds of human meddlers.

But quite the opposite is true. The place exists because the people who have passed here before us have wished it into being. Otherwise, the site would be in shambles; the pottery shards, discarded. Here… here are the shards for you to see. Pick them up, feel the grooves in your fingers. Run your hands along the walls we built to shield us from the wind.

No one tells them to do it. But year after year, the curators—silent, nameless, unknown— come and go. All that remains of them are messy cairns and an odd footstep in the sand.

§

On our way out we happened upon a panel of petroglyphs, etched into almost burnt-black sandstone. It featured animal tracks, big birds with wings outstretched, human and non-human heads. Spiraling shapes drew my nose inches from the rock, as if a closer look could explain how ancient artists chiseled precise curves into solid rock with little more than a pointed end. It didn't make sense. The panel was otherworldly, yet incomplete. Half the panel had sheared and fallen off. Bullet holes littered the rock face. Dry cowpies littered the foreground beyond a sagging cable and a dilapidated sign that read NO FOOT TRAFFIC BEYOND THIS POINT.

How do you preserve a place? Do you put up walls around the walls to deny time, hide from the wind? Do you charge entry to areas deemed culturally relevant, and use the money to staff a curator, an expert in the field, to speak to guests about what it all means? Is naming, identifying, putting a place on a map the key to its preservation? Mark Twain came to know the Mississippi as he knew "the letters of the alphabet…" In that process, something changed for the author, and for the river: the "grace, beauty, and poetry" vanished from its waters. Knowledge leached in, took their place.

It may have behooved Twain to read some Heraclitus, who quipped, millennia earlier, that "you cannot step twice in the same river." Rivers themselves go out to sea, or turn into trickles, or dive under the earth, or dry up.[2] The sun bares down, even on *nahodish-gish*, a Navajo term meaning "places to be left alone." Wind, that

---

[2] Jorge Manrique wrote, *"nuestras vidas son los ríos / que van a dar a la mar, / que es el morir."* "Our lives are the rivers / that race out to the sea, / where they cease to be."

tireless sculptor, goes to work. The bell tolls for everything that is matter, for places, for the meanings we affectionately lay on them, for us.

We are stubborn and may not like it. So, we lean into the wind. We focus on units that make sense: "the next generation." We take them there, tell them stories, write about it, convincing ourselves we've bided a bit more time. Even amidst this spare landscape that is guaranteed to resemble a barren wasteland on Google Maps there are colors that require more than one word to describe. And yet… this beating place and the characters that fill it up will simply and irrevocably disappear. I suppose I need temporary shelter from that truth. Maybe the old artists and builders of this place did too. The impulse to preserve exists out of that tension—to love what is and to fear what could be lost.

§

Hours before setting out on that slickrock, we called our host. We had rolled into town early and wanted to know her recommendations for local hikes. "Yeah, we don't really like to give out names," she said, her voice trailing off. None of us knew it at the time, but the comment freed us to have an experience.

We put our finger on an old map: not too close, not too far from town. We missed the turn, had to drive back. We navigated divots on that dirt road, eschewing lanes, wondering if there would be enough clearance underneath the car. We parked (we thought) at the spot we had pointed to on the map. It could have been another place. We didn't know any better.

And I am better off for it. A towhee and I locked eyes. A single fly shuttled from rock to rock in noisy defiance against the almost-void of a desert winter. For a moment, a glistening lithic sea enveloped me. And a strange gravity compelled me to take a seat and drink in the color, the silence, the communion, and the fragility of a place that will remain without a name.

Aidan Gaughran has called the Four Corners home for three years. In the seven years prior, he lived in various places abroad, where he learned to listen and marvel at the thin line that exists between the magic and the real.

· P O E M ·

Your Location Could Not Be Determined

David Feela

The last time I checked
moonlight glazed the desert white.
There at the side of the road
I tapped out an informal Morse code
against the steering wheel
but nothing was wrong.
I had shut off the engine
and opened my windows
to hear the tick of the cooling earth.
I was both on my way and not
trying anymore, my lungs
emptied and refreshed
like spring water issuing from the ground
with no more purpose than to
wash the bedrock clean.
Of the shadows around me

some shaped themselves
into hogans where the faint stars
sat in their ancient circles

David Feela's writing has appeared in hundreds of regional and national publications, including the High Country News, Mountain Gazette D, Small Farmer's Journal, Utne Reader, and The Denver Post. Published collections consist of three poetry volumes, a Colorado Book Award finalist collection of essays, and a massive chain of online links. He lives in Cortez, Colorado and his website can be viewed @ feelasophy.weebly.com

Not the Superstitious Sort

Josh Jones

If Jessie Crade were the superstitious sort, he'd reckon the town was haunted. It was a mess of burned out buildings, nothing but charred timber and rusted tin. The only structures still standing were the orphanage and a sad little chapel, and although the orphanage was what he sought, he was most interested in the crumbling well in the center of town. He hoped to hell there was a drink of water in it.

He peered down inside, nudged a loose stone over the edge, and wasn't surprised to hear a thump instead of a splash. No luck here. He tried to spit into the well to share his disgust, but his mouth was too dry. He leaned against the beam that once held a bucket winch and rubbed the back of his sunburnt neck.

"What in the hell now, Jim?" he asked, uncrumpling the map to study it again, as if doing so would shed new light on his current predicament. The town and the orphanage were drawn on it, and so was the mine entrance, which looked to lie further south. His brother's ugly scrawl might say exactly how to find the mine, but Jessie had never learned his letters. It made his head hurt to look at words he couldn't read. He squinted around at the orphanage, at the chapel, at the husk of a town. Doubtful that anyone was living here, and that dried his plans right up. He'd never had much luck in life, and his hopes of finding anyone here to read his brother's map to him were looking sunk. He'd need to find some shade until the sun wasn't so high and think about what to do next.

The town proper offered no respite, and the orphanage looked set to collapse. Patches of whitewash flaked from crumbling adobe walls, and tumbleweeds choked every corner. The building was all sagging lintels and gaping windows, and the entire rear of it listed to one side. He guessed that just tugging the front door might bring the whole thing down.

The chapel was run down too, but not as bad. Its front door was hanging by one hinge, and the steeple had toppled clean over, leaving a jagged hole in the roof. But all the windows were shuttered from the sun, and the structure looked sound. He guessed he could steal some shade inside without it collapsing on top of his head.

He ducked through the loose door and was shocked at how cold it was inside the vestibule. It wasn't a welcome cold, even after the heat outside. It dug into his bones, and he started shivering just a few steps in. He heard scratching sounds, like rats scraping around in the walls, that made his ears hurt. His guts twisted like he'd had a bowl of bad beans, and he swayed forward, burping a string of sick onto the floor.

"Damn you, Jim," he said. "Wasted your last breath telling me about this orphanage when you shoulda just told me what words you wrote on your map."

He stumbled his way into the chapel's nave. It was dark as a cave inside, even with sunlight slanting through the hole in the roof. He meant to lay on a pew until his sickness passed, but just as quick as it started, the sickness stopped. He felt good enough to start cursing his brother all over again, but he got off track when he saw a nun glowing in that halo of slanting light.

She was seated at a desk, dressed in a white habit, her pale face turned down to her folded hands, like she was praying. A blackboard covered in white scribbles stood behind her. The pews had been pushed against the walls, making room for neat rows of little desks. Jessie could just make out the small shapes of seated children, their heads bent low over slate boards, scratching away with bits of chalk.

There were no ghosts in this town. Just a sad looking Sister, teaching some kids their lessons.

The floor creaked as he stepped further in, and all at once, the children stopped writing. The Sister looked up at the new arrival.

"We have a visitor."

She was a pretty one, even with her sad, pale face. None of the children turned round. Just started whispering to each other instead.

"Water," he croaked, and she gestured to a bowl on a rough-cut table beneath a faded icon of God's Eye. He fell to his knees, stuck his face in the bowl, and lapped at the water like a dog. He'd never had such a delicious drink; might even have offered a prayer of thanks if he'd had anything else to be thankful for. Instead he undid the dirty cloth tied round his neck, sopped out the dregs, and mopped his face before turning back to the Sister.

"My brother Jim was foreman at that mine south of here. He said Sister Rachel hired out orphans to him to work the claim. I'd like to hire one for myself."

The whispering stopped, and the Sister's face went slack. She was painfully bright in the sunlight, almost too much for him to look at.

"Sister Rachel is gone. These children are no longer for sale."

"Here now, I ain't tryin to buy one." He kept his voice low and calm. "I never learned to read, see, and I just need someone to help me with some words my brother wrote. He left something at that mine he wanted me to have. That was his dying wish."

"The mine is cursed by God. Death is all you will find there," replied the Sister.

Jessie didn't believe in God or curses. Seemed the Sister was going to make trouble for him, and he was already tired of it. If she didn't want to help, well then, he'd help himself.

"Here now, Sister." He took a step toward the nearest desk. "I'm glad to donate to your cause, how does that sound?" He would just snatch one of these kids up and show his knife if the Sister wouldn't cooperate. "I just need some words read, and help finding that mine. Ain't y'all here to help?" He sidled a step closer. "I'll pay you, only after. Don't you want some gold to fix up your orphanage?"

"We don't need gold."

"You don't . . . Now Sister, who don't need any gold?"

"These children suffered in that mine because of a Sister's greed for gold."

"I don't aim to harm no kids."

"Your brother promised the same."

"I shouldn't be held liable for my brother's doings, those years ago. You refusing me, Sister?"

"These children serve God now. If any choose of their own accord to serve Him by helping you, I will not protest."

Holy proclamations made Jessie's mind curdle, and he was done talking. He reached for the shirt scruff of a towheaded boy seated in the back row.

"I'll serve, Sister."

The small voice came from the front, and a dark shape moved into the light. It was a Mesoli girl dressed in a black burlap frock, and she was the ugliest little thing Jessie had ever seen. The side of her face looked stoved in, like someone had hit her with a rock. Her left brow was dented, and the eye underneath was squinched closed. Her cheek drooped like candle wax. Her good eye was gray, bright against her dark skin.

Jessie found it hard to stomach her ugliness, but he liked it best when things weren't trouble. This one would work just as well as any, so he swaggered over and handed her the map.

"Property of Jim Crade," she read, and turned her one good eye to Jessie. He pointed to the mine drawn on the map, and to the words beside it.

"Does it tell how to get there?"

"Yes, Mr. Jim."

He looked to the Sister. "Well, then. Girl's willing to help, even if you ain't."

"And God will reward her for it."

He looked down at the ugly dirtskin.

"How far?" he asked.

"A day's walk."

Jessie squinted out the chapel door. Too hot to go now, and he wanted some rest first.

"Get me some water." He handed the girl his empty skin. "And food." He sneered back at the Sister, expecting a fuss, but she was just staring at her hands, with that same sad face as before. Couldn't blame her, stuck in this sorry town with this sorry clutch of kids. Especially this one, maybe the sorriest of the lot, with her broken face.

"Well? Go on now."

"Yes, Mr. Jim."

"Jim's my brother, girl. This was his map, that's why his name's on it. You ain't that smart, are you? Even with all your schooling." He surveyed the room. The rest of the kids were sitting still in their rows, their heads bowed like the Sister's. "That's good, y'all keep praying. No more scratching with your chalk. I got me some shut-eye to get."

He collapsed onto a pew, satisfied with these developments. He'd gotten help without too much trouble. It wasn't clear how this sorry bunch was still alive in this dead-ass town, but that wasn't his concern, way he saw it. There was plenty of churches around, and Sister could get help from one of her own if she needed it.

He woke in darkness, his mouth dry as dirt. Couldn't remember where he was. He scrambled up to a sit, looking around wildly, and nearly called out for help until he saw the Mesoli girl sitting cross-legged in a pool of moonlight.

His heart was jumping like it might blow out. He leaned forward, mopping sweat and clutching his chest. He'd been dreaming about shoveling dirt into a shallow grave, onto his brother Jim's body. Then it was suddenly him in the grave, and it was Jim burying him, except he was alive instead of dead. He kept calling out for his brother to please stop, but every time he opened his mouth to holler, Jim scooped dirt into it.

"Just thirsty's all," he said. The girl was watching him with that one good eye, worrying a little pendant that dangled from her neck. "The hell you staring at? Gimme that."

He snatched it from her, breaking the chain. Gave it a good look. It was a church icon, an etching of God's Eye, nearly rubbed clean off. He'd been hoping it was made of silver, which he'd have kept for himself, for his trouble, but it was pewter, so he tossed it to the floor. She grabbed it and stowed it in her pocket.

"It's a good night for travel, Mr. Jim." She handed Jessie his water skin and he grabbed it from her and sucked at it like a calf on a tit.

"I said food, too. Y'all been eating on something, ain't you?"

She passed him a hunk of frybread. He took a bite, but found it hard to swallow down.

"Tastes like dirt," he said. "Let's just get."

The girl was right, it was a good night for travel. It was cool but not cold, and the moon gave plenty of light by which to see. She led them south and somewhat east, on a straight course through stunted mesquites and scattered yuccas. He kept thinking about his dream. Why was he getting buried alive? He'd been the one who'd done the burying, and his brother was dead when he did it. He knew that for a fact, as he had put his own knife into Jim's heart.

"Should've had him read his map to me first, then I wouldn't have to trouble with you."

"Yes, Mr. Jim."

"You stupid or something? I already told you, Jim's my brother." Whatever knock she'd taken to her noggin must've softened her thoughts. "Guess you worked that claim for him. Must be why you keep confusing us, everyone said we favored one another. He do that to your face?"

A nod.

"Sounds like him. Meanest bastard I ever knew. Well, I'm meaner'n he was, so smarten up, or I'll make you uglier still."

They walked all through the morning. The sun crept higher, leaning on Jessie with a fury. He'd normally like a rest during the worst heat, but he wanted his gold even more, so he pushed them on. They got to the foothills at dusk, and it wasn't but a few twists and turns through a canyon before they got to the mine, its entrance gaping like an empty eye socket.

"What does this say?" He pointed at the map. The girl read to him which lefts and rights to take through the tunnels.

"Well, after you."

"It's haunted in there, Mr. Jim."

"I don't believe in ghosts."

Jessie was not the superstitious sort, and this dirtskin wasn't going to scare him. He nudged her through the entrance. There was a crate of torches, and he took a bundle, lighting one. The tunnels were stone and dirt, with rotten beams holding it all in place. And it was powerful cold inside.

"This whole place could be set to cave in, so don't touch nothing. I don't mean to get buried alive."

"Yes, Mr. Jim."

It didn't take long for Jessie to get turned around. Tunnels kept branching off, and each one looked the same as the last. Soon their route opened onto a cavern, with a black pit at its center.

"Eyes open, ain't no ground here."

He tossed his dying torch down into the pit, and the shadows of leering skulls and grasping hands jittered around the walls. At the bottom was a deadfall of bones and dried skin, of crooked little necks and broken spines and black burlap frocks. Draped on top of the pile of small corpses was a woman dressed in crisp church white. Her head was twisted around backwards, grinning up at Jessie.

"Looks like Sister Rachel is gone alright. Guess Jim didn't want to trouble with paying her out. Let's get, or I'll toss you down there too." The girl watched the torch burn out, her expression blank as the pile of orphans was swallowed up by blackness.

They skirted the hole and entered the tunnel opposite. She led them, left and right, right and left, until they came to the final turn.

"Thirty-two paces. Hole at crossbeam. Under black rock," she read.

He paced out the steps, held his torch up to the crossbeam. There was a wide crack running its length, and sure enough, a hole in the ceiling above it. The hole was just big enough for a child to fit through.

Before his brother had died, Jessie made him tell how he'd hidden his gold. How he'd sent a kid up in that hole to stash it inside. Said the girl he put up there had an accident, so Jessie would have to find himself another. Well, he'd found one that would fit just right. He lit another torch and tossed the dying one up through the hole.

"Get on my shoulders, and watch that broken beam!" Up she

scrambled, and Jessie called after her. "You see the black rock?"

"Yes," she said. He heard the scrape of shifted stone, followed by a small cry and a clatter of wood.

"My torch went out, Mr. Jim! I'm afraid of the dark!" There was a tumble of rocks, a scream, a wet smack. He raised his own torch to the hole, poking it around as grit rained down.

"Follow my light, girl!"

". . . torch went out . . ." She sounded far away, and Jessie started to fret. What if she got lost up there with his gold? He'd have to go all the way back to town for another kid.

". . . Mr. Jim . . ." drifted down, and a cold wind followed.

"Drop it here!" He reached his torch as high as he could, and soon a large bundle of frayed burlap fell out, landing in front of him.

". . . afraid of the dark . . ." This time she sounded closer. Jessie figured he'd just leave her up there if she didn't stop fooling around. He stabbed his torch into the dirt floor and fumbled with the burlap, looking for the opening. It didn't weigh nothing, and felt like kindling was stuffed inside.

"What's this? Where's my gold?"

He brought the sack closer to the torch, saw something poking out the top. It was a small skull, its jawbone swinging loosely, like it was laughing at him. Its forehead was dented, an eye socket crushed, its face broken. A chain hung from its neck, a pewter pendant, with an etching of God's Eye, worn smooth from the tiny thumb that had worried it so.

Jessie's hands started to shake, and little bones trickled from the sack. Not a sack, he saw, but a black burlap frock. He whimpered at the ugly skull, and God help him, its one good eye hole was staring back at him.

". . . Torch went out, Mr. Jim . . . I'm afraid of the dark . . ." And this time a shriek came up from one end of the tunnel and howled down the other.

He turned a full circle, strewing bones around him, as the shriek echoed back and forth, back and forth.

"...dark...Jim...dark...Jim..."

A louder scream twined with it, and Jessie realized it was coming from him. He dropped the Mesoli girl, tripped over her bones, landed against a support beam, and heard a crack. A rush of sand filled his mouth, cutting off his scream, and he felt the pounding of pebble and stone, and the crushing, crushing darkness.

Josh Jones was born and raised in Harrison, Arkansas, and graduated from the University of Arkansas with a Master's degree in Geography. He and his wife live off-grid in their RV, and can be found in Durango, Colorado in the summer, southern Arizona in the winter, and traveling the Four Corners states during the seasons between. He is releasing a novella soon, and has a novel in the works.

· P O E M ·

Alpine Epiphany

William R. Morris

Resting
On a granite slab left by a retreating glacier
At the shallow edge of an alpine lake.
Scents of spruce and fir mingle
With the harsh complaint of a Steller's jay.
Heartbeat slowing, my eyes adjust through polarized lenses.

Looking
Mid-depth into the placid turquoise water,
Hanging languid a cutthroat trout.
Pulsing gills, liquid breath,
Iridescent flanks of colors seen in ring-necked pheasants or dreamt
by forest sprites,
Shimmering sunlight captured on the fish-skin canvas.

Pondering
A younger man's trophy
Evolving into a mature meeting of fellow creatures,
Allowing each the silent grace of this encounter.
Immediacy races to permanent experience,
Memory eclipsing life.

Realizing
The sacred truth of now,
A sacrament to be shared, not hoarded.
Love lived, incarnate.
Trout and human,
Breathing and being.

William R. Morris, National Park Service Ranger turned United Methodist Pastor, has explored and shared some amazing wilderness parks: Denali, Grand Canyon, Everglades, and Mesa Verde. He's a lifelong traveler, interpreter of Creation, advocate of public lands, and avid hiker. Will, Jane, and their dog, Nutmeg, live just outside of Cortez.

July Light

Amy Grogan

Emerald alpine slopes are accented by darker clumps of willow and krummolz—stunted, twisted pine trees that survive at 11,500 feet. Drier ocher patches create a mosaic in a variegated palette rolling down to the water's edge. A blast of wind approaches from the opposite shore turning the rippling water to a darker slate blue. I can see it coming full bore seconds before I hear it or feel it. Then stillness again and the lake returns to its former self of mini lapping waves. With the higher arc of a July sun, this high alpine lake, the largest of a trio, reflects as a deeper grey blue with chocolate sand edging. To the right, a remnant snowbank hangs a few feet above the water on the cooler north face. I am perched on the western edge on top of granite bedrock streaked with quartz lines of white running over a steep drop-off. Dwarf willow are interspersed with orange red paintbrush and fuchsia elephant head flowers. Not many wildflowers are growing above tree line this dry year, but I cherish this splash of color regardless.

Spring this year was erratic with hot dry steady winds following a drier winter. Other than some moisture in December, the rest of the season was lackluster for snowpack. Then strong spring winds barreled in and did not let up until recently. In the last week more consistent moisture returned, to everyone's relief. A visitor would not realize the level of dryness down lower in elevation where chest high, bright blue delphiniums line up in rows. But it is shadier down there, where towering trees hold the moisture. With the spread of the spruce beetle die off, this patch of forest has been hit hard. Not many large green trees remain.

On the hike up, I revisit a spot at tree line that I painted twenty years ago called Highland Cascade. Today I want to compare those trees with how they look now. They're completely dead. Their peculiar angle caught my eye back then, but the focus of the painting was the cascading water, which has not changed. Fortunately, I note now that the younger spruce seem unaffected by the beetle and are still green and thriving. The forest will not be wiped out entirely. For the rest of my lifetime these forests will be markedly different, probably sparser. Maybe a smaller forest will attract more wildlife. Or maybe less.

More clouds roll in overhead, but there's only a thirty percent chance of rain today so I stay up high. With my dog, Jolly, I linger in this glorious day. Northeast winds have picked up causing the amplitude of the waves to increase and crash below. The color of the lake has changed to a brighter slate blue that contrasts with the brown mud.

One year, Charlie and I ventured over to the seldom visited eastern shore of this lake to explore a spit of sand. It is always a good idea to change one's perspective and see the light on the lake from an unfamiliar angle. We climbed the hills to a high point at ridge line, hoping to spot the South Fork Fire. It wasn't difficult. A towering plume of smoke topped an enormous cumulus cloud with orange red tinting on the underside. The fire looked to be generating its own weather pattern. It was both magnificent and horrible to watch.

Today, clouds stack up and rain is falling to the northeast, but it may not be making it to the ground. The lake's mood changes as shadows from the clouds blanket it, backed by a stiff wind. This summer seems to be the year of the wind.

Jolly and I move on, climbing in a southwest trajectory to a ridge line where we're surrounded by sunny dwarf sunflowers, six to eight inches tall. One of my favorites, their heads are all turned to face the sun. Above and in the distance, lofty thirteen-thousand-foot peaks shoot straight up in a dizzying tower of granite. Below, the lakes tuck into a low spot surrounded by higher hills. The lake is fed by thin waterfalls spilling over grey volcanic cliff bands to the west and, depending on the light, can be transformed into purple mountain's majesty. It is a coveted spot for hikers and backpackers for the water, views, and abundance of wildflowers.

This year seems sparse in comparison to last year when a huge March snowstorm led to acres of jaw-dropping wildflowers. Everything above tree line was blanketed by deep snow until the end of July. Charlie and I hiked up here the last week of August and the color show was on, but it was unprecedented for its lateness. I shot the equivalent of three to four rolls of film.

Jolly and I have picked another place to linger—a huge but shallow pond. Some people may consider this a lake, but I categorize lakes as having depth. Private and off the main trail, I prefer this secret spot. Wildflowers around the lake boast yellow tints. Lemon yellow flowers that look similar to paintbrush are interspersed with smaller, unnamed flowers of a deeper marigold hue. Lower in the duff emerge tiny purple heather, topped off with creamy snowballs of bistort. This plant has the sense of being suspended in the air. Their tiny stems camouflage into the ground, so their fluffy white heads appear to float. The pond surface is an acid green with ocher sand underneath. Quite different than the huge, blue lakes nearby. I am surrounded by a ring of more dwarf willow from which I hear a high pitched *peet, peet, peet,* but not revealing itself. On the edge of the shore where it is wet, more elephant heads with their distinct flower petal arrangement, looking similar to an elephant's trunk. Hot pink Parry Primrose dot the wetland areas with the boldest color out here.

And then I stumble on a gem: a white alabaster perfectly crenellated sculpture of snow dusted with pink algae on top. At each fold and carved out ridge is an outline smudged with black lines, giving the structure a very graphite look. The middle snow sculpture is a long island flanked by two creeks on either side. Fins stretch out to form an outdoor land-based piece that surpasses anything created by the most talented human sculptors. To my left, the center massive, probably fifty feet long, almost touching where it terminates with its neighbor, the sculpture ends in a thick fin that looks so delicate it could cave in instantly. But when I touch these thinner edges I realize the snow is supportive and strong. This had to have been left over from an avalanche, maybe even two winters before, what has now been referred to as the Big Winter. Two successive snowstorms barreled into our area a year ago in March and left behind snow paths and a pack so deep, the county was buried in concrete above tree line for months into the summer.

Finding a hidden organic treasure such as this alters my perspective to the landscape into one of unforeseen possibilities. If this piece can somehow survive without any human mark for two years in a popular place, it gives me hope. Maybe it's more of a commentary about humans in general. We tend to be followers and stick to the trail, rather than explorers, off on one's own. Probably no one cares. Clearly, it is the artist in me that elevates a snowbank into something else. I have done this since I was a kid. Observing the outdoors and imagining objects in the landscape into something else.

On our hike back to the trailhead we descend past the lakes from this morning over creeks and unstable talus to the forest below. Lush stands of *Mertensia,* Rocky Mountain bluebells, in variegated hues of blues to pinks are everywhere. Their leaves are edible with a distinct pungency. Wild geranium, orange sneezeweed, rosy crown, pink asters and pink paintbrush fill in the blanks. Deep purple to sapphire blue delphiniums dominate a foot and a half tall above the other flowering plants in lush pockets here and there. A shade of rare blue so uncommon in these mountains that it grabs your attention instantly. Crops of huge, green folded stalks of corn lilies with no showy flowers at all make their monochromatic stance counterpoint to their exuberant flowering neighbors. The landscape is blanketed by a cornucopia of plant life, each with its own distinct patterns, textures and colors. My perception of the plants, rocks, water and trees changes by how the light is affecting the landscape at different times of the day. Ultimately, these impressions will find their way into my artwork. It's one of the reasons why I venture out into the mountains in the summer. Flower season and the milder weather is so brief at this high elevation that I could miss it if I did not set aside days to witness the bold expression.

Amy Grogan is a relief printmaker and writer who has lived in Southwest Colorado for 32 years. Her forthcoming book, Aspens Alive, *which she has block printed and written, is expected to be published in 2025. Her submission, "July Light" is one month in "A Year of Light," an artist's written and illustrated perspective of the Southwestern landscape.*

2024: A Total Eclipse

Mimi Gorman

Today was about darkness:
the moon passing in front of the sun.

Tonight is about light:
an expansive sphere
carrying the heat of today
and forever's awakenings
as it slides in silence
past the horizon,
holding steadfast
with fading luminescence.

"Let go," the sun offers.
Let go.

Mimi Gorman has worked and lived several seasons in Colorado. She is finally a full-time resident of Mancos. Writing, surveying bumblebees, birding, and exploring museums and landscapes fill her days.

Sufficient Unto the Day

Grace Morledge

They had planned to be married on April 1 in the office of the county clerk, but a freak snowstorm nearly stopped the show. Fortunately, Horace had ordered a taxi in which to pick up his prospective bride – an indulgence, for they both always either walked or took the bus. When the cab arrived at her door, just as the first fat flakes were streaming sideways, Rachel stood in the hallway wearing a modest blue flowered dress, a cloth coat, open-toed pumps, and galoshes. She believed in being prepared for anything. She picked up a muffler and gloves and shoved open the swollen door of the shotgun cottage she shared with her mother. Creaking and screeching, the underdog house contended gamely with the wind.

"There you are!" Horace shouted, leaning across the seat to open the taxi door. She swung her damp boots inside and turned to him. Horace was stocky and short, but he had the most beautiful eyes of any mortal man; eyes she had fallen for behind his teller's cage.

They were round and green and long-lashed and sparkling, today more with anger than with premarital joy. "This is going to be the trip of a lifetime." He often sounded sarcastic and kind of unhappy, but she put up with it for the sake of being his girl.

"Did you bring the bouquet?"

"Oh, yes." Horace picked up a bundle of daisies from the seat beside him and thrust it at her. "You'd look beautiful, darling, were it not that your hair is mussed and you're dressed for the Klondike." Horace himself was wearing his best suit without an overcoat and his black banking oxfords with just a pair of rubber overshoes to protect the shine.

"Thank you, Ducks." Rachel smiled as if he'd produced a great compliment. Remembering himself, he gave her a quick peck on the lips.

"It's gonna be a slow trip to the courthouse," said the cabbie as the meter turned over with a clunk.

"Just so we're moving. I don't much like paying to sit still, unless there's a movie on."

The cabbie grunted and turned the big steering wheel, aiming his Checker through the crunching snow. A whiteout was beginning. Cigar smoke crept over the seatback and into the black well where Rachel's knees and Horace's bent formally, side by side. Drunken riders on the night before had strewn wine-stained paper cups across the floor alongside the crusts of Automat sandwiches wrapped in waxed paper. "Pigs," said Horace. "Taxis are plain unsanitary."

Watching dark sedans lumber towards them through the moving curtain of the windshield wipers, Rachel clutched her bouquet.

"Look out!" Horace shrieked. A delivery van bore down on them, and the taxi spun at a waltz tempo, arcing across the glassy street and onto the opposite curb. Rachel's forehead hit the front seat, and her flowers landed head-first on the floor. Horace gasped. "Do you have snow tires on this heap, or just bald rubber?"

The cabbie thrust back a plaid wool elbow, flicking cigar ash onto Rachel's knee. "In case you hadn't noticed, it's a blizzard, buddy. Keep your pants on. I'll get you there."

And he did. It was the worst kind of start to the worst kind of day she'd ever failed to imagine, but she'd learned something, Rachel later thought.

When they fell separately into the revolving door, the snow was ankle deep. Rachel pushed ahead, leaning on the brass bar until she stumbled into the courthouse foyer, stamping her feet behind Horace, who was doused in a dandruff of snow. "I wish I'd brought us an umbrella," Rachel said, brushing his shoulders. She felt nervous as she held up the bouquet with three of its daisy heads dejectedly bent. She sighed.

"This way." Horace hurried her up the marble stairs. Once inside the registry office, they spotted a bored lady at a counter who had them sign the marriage book, and Rachel removed the triplicate blood test forms from her purse.

"You're the first business we've had today," said the lady, not unkindly. "For some people love can't compete with a snowstorm, but not for you two, I guess." She smiled. Rachel smiled back. "The justice of the peace is finishing his cigarette. Did you bring a witness, or will you need one?"

"I guess we'll need one," said Rachel.

"Luke's coming," said Horace, dusting his sleeves. He cleared his throat.

"Luke Frazier?"

"Yeah. He offered." Horace's plump cheeks were flushed with cold. She peered hopefully into his lovely green eyes just as Luke himself entered – tall and dark with deep-black eyes above his muffler. Luke took her cold hand in his. "You look lovely, my friend."

His earnest gaze made Rachel feel grateful for the first time that day. Sometimes she wished for a man with Horace's captivating eyes and Luke's kindly way of seeing her. It was not to be, she supposed.

"Do you have the ring?" Luke asked.

"Oh, yeah." Horace explored his breast pockets until he produced a plain gold band. It looked too big for Rachel's finger.

"So what now?" Luke asked. "There's nobody here." The counter lady had left the room, and the justice of the peace was still nowhere in sight.

"Guess we wait," Horace replied. The three of them piled onto a wooden pew, with Horace in the middle, Rachel on one end, and Luke on the other. We must look a fright, Rachel thought. She lifted her feet one at a time and pulled the wet galoshes off, exposing her spring shoes. She set her boots neatly beside a hat tree where she hung her cloth coat and muffler.

Luke and Horace removed their fedoras, as if they'd just remembered that gentlemen take their hats off indoors. Luke patted Horace's knee. "Don't be nervous."

"It's all right, Ducks," said Rachel, dropping her own hand gently onto the remaining knee. "Once the ceremony's over, you can get back to work and I'll go break the news to Mother." She wouldn't be living with Horace right away, not until they found an apartment they could afford. Rachel had considered leaving her mother in the dark for a while but decided the wedding ring would attract suspicion. She knew it was bad luck to take her ring off once the groom had placed it on her finger. She watched Horace shake the golden loop in his right hand like a die. Outside the mullioned windows, the snow fell even faster than before.

"Good morning!"

All three of them jumped as a small, portly man in a shiny brown suit and wide silk tie slipped through a half door in the counter. His yellowed white hair crossed his pate in several oily lines. He looked from Luke to Horace and back. "Which one of you is the groom?"

"I," Horace choked. "I am."

"Well, very pleased to meet you, Mister . . ."

"Ridley," Luke interjected.

"I'm Judge Hawthorne, the JP," the little man said, reaching up companionably to pat Horace on the back. "Don't be nervous. Come with me. There's a special room we use for weddings. It's a little more private in there."

Rachel followed her mid-sized groom and his tall friend through a narrow hallway. Formally holding her wrinkled bouquet, she paced evenly behind the men, feeling oddly like a third wheel at her own wedding. Despite the lovely eyes, the dinners at Carl's Cafe, the movie matinees with his arm about her shoulders before she had to hurry home to her mother, Rachel felt that everything – and nothing—was about to change. Her shoulders sagged. Her lips began to tremble.

The tiny room contained a few wooden office chairs, an old panoramic photo of the city, and an oak lectern. The sole window alcove was plastered shut, blocking any natural light. The counter lady shook Judge Hawthorne's black robe and stooped to help him slide his arms into the sleeves. Grinning, he gripped the lectern below his chest and pulled a well-worn card from his vest pocket before he laid his suit jacket neatly on a chair.

"Any questions before we get started?" he asked.

"Where do we stand?" Horace replied.

"We're ready to go. I've got the vows right here." Hawthorne raised his card and grinned again. Horace's round cheeks grew redder.

"No, *how* do we stand. I mean, in what order?"

"Best man and groom to the left," said counter lady. "And you on the right, my dear. Since you don't have a girlfriend here, I can stand up with you if you want." She smiled at Rachel, who felt somewhat mollified.

"I'd like that," she said.

The four of them arranged themselves like children lining up. Rachel glanced at Horace, but she could see only his neatly shaved neck and his bald spot, for he had turned his face toward Luke. She attempted to meet Luke's dark eyes, but they were fixed on his friend with an expression of concern. Rachel knew Horace tended toward anxiety, but she had never seen him quite this upset. She laid her hand lightly on his shoulder blade and he flinched but did not turn to her.

Judge Hawthorne cleared his throat. "Well," he said. "I'll be starting with you, future Mrs. Ridley. Ladies first, you know. I'll read the vow and then you respond, 'I do,' all right?" She nodded. "Then I'll do the same with Mr. Ridley. He'll answer, 'I do,' and then I'll call for dissenters, and then I'll ask for the ring, and then a little kiss and we're done."

"What do you mean, dissenters?" Horace growled.

"Just a formality," said Hawthorne and turned to Rachel, who stood up straight with her daisies drooping proudly before her. "Do you, Rachel Randolph, take this man to be your lawfully wedded husband, in sickness and in health, and, forsaking all others, cleave only unto him so long as you both shall live?" He looked expectantly up at Rachel.

"I do," she answered clearly. She glanced at Horace as a drop of perspiration descended his carefully shaven cheek.

"Do you, Horace Ridley, take this woman to be your lawfully wedded wife, in sickness and in health, and, forsaking all others, cleave only unto her so long as you both shall live?"

There was a pause during which Rachel heard Horace swallow twice and clear his throat.

"I do," he said, but it sounded as if he were confessing to a crime. Rachel replaced her solemn look with a slight smile and tried to meet his eyes, but Horace was staring at the floor.

"Now," said Hawthorne, speeding his pace. "If anyone here knows a reason why this man and this woman should not be joined in matrimony let him speak now or forever hold his peace. See, I said it was a formality. Could I have the ring please?"

Rachel felt a flush begin in the center of her chest and rise slowly upward to her hairline where her neatly set pin curls grew suddenly damp with sweat. Gently, the counter lady lifted the ruined bouquet from her hands. A silent moment passed. She saw Luke turn her groom's left hand over and place the gold band on his palm. It shone in the light of the ceiling lamp, round as a brass faucet washer and nearly as large. He closed the man's fingers over it.

"I can't," Horace said almost inaudibly. "It's a lie." He turned to Luke, whose black eyes panicked. He pulled Luke toward him by the left hand, then jammed the ring onto Luke's third finger, where it fit. He then grasped Luke by the ears and kissed him, hard, upon the lips.

Rachel's eyes grew wide. The counter lady dropped the bouquet, and it rolled beneath an office chair. Horace turned and staggered to the wedding room door, wrenching it open. Incongruously, Rachel noticed that he had not taken the rubbers off his shoes. Empty-handed, she looked to Luke for explanation or comfort.

"I'm sorry, Rachel." He looked extremely uncomfortable, either wounded or embarrassed. "I'll go and straighten him out," he said.

The world was suddenly full of harsh sentences; the condemnation of few words. Rachel flexed her chilled hands and looked at them, at their long fingers and short but carefully manicured nails. She was beyond embarrassment. The dutiful witness lady put an arm around her shoulders, maybe to comfort her or to keep her from falling. Rachel, however, was steady on her feet. Her face had shed its solemn smile and formed a primitive mask: teeth exposed, nose wrinkled, eyes narrowed. "Don't cry, honey. This happens sometimes."

"I'm not going to cry," said Rachel firmly. She had just now realized that she was not.

"If you want, I can see that your fiancé is charged with sodomy and breach of contract," said the JP, abandoning his jocund tone. Rachel jumped. She had forgotten him.

"Oh, no. That won't be necessary."

The lady handed her the discarded bouquet, then slipped the judicial robe off Hawthorne's shoulders. With a deep breath, he shrugged into his jacket. "Suit yourself," he said.

Turning the metal doorknob, Rachel strode with purpose back to the registry office. The men's hats were gone but her own coat and galoshes awaited her patiently. Brilliant sunshine sliced the dust that floated in the air of the room; the storm had ended, and outside the window the fresh snow sparkled like rock salt. Rachel walked to the wire trash bin to deposit her flowers.

"April Fool," she said. She no longer felt ashamed, although it seemed as if she ought to. She felt, instead, strangely easy.

"Can I call you a cab?" asked the counter lady.

"No thank you. I'll be fine." She sat to buckle on her galoshes, tied the plaid muffler around her neck like a cravat, neatly buttoned her coat, and pulled on her black leather gloves as might a woman of means. She straightened her back and left the office.

Outside, a county custodian slowly scraped the sidewalk clear. Beyond his grating coal shovel, the street looked slippery as a block of ice. Rachel doubted the buses were running. She walked along the sidewalk, her small boot prints among the first to break the fresh snow. She was glad she had worn the serious galoshes and not the translucent covers meant to latch over a woman's high heels. Stopping at a news stand, she bought the morning paper from a solitary vendor who was hugging himself and exhaling foggy breaths. She sucked in the crisp morning air and set off for home, feeling the light like an unexpected gift.

When Rachel approached her little underdog house, its porch roof was toothy with icicles. The old place had weathered the storm. She set her galoshes neatly on the mat and hung her wet outerwear from the hall tree to dry. Then she walked into the living room, sat down on the velveteen divan, and spread the paper open before her to the tiny column of classified ads listed under "Jobs for Women." A compact figure, she laced her hands together quietly in thought.

"Rachel! Where *have* you been?" Her mother emerged from the back porch shaking a string mop that had frozen while drying outdoors. "Gracious, I couldn't imagine. I thought maybe you'd been kidnapped."

Rachel studied the woman – her paunch expanding the navy dress, a cameo brooch linking the lace above her bosom, her ridiculous dyed red hair. Without warning, Rachel burst out laughing; deep, unladylike belly laughs that left her sobbing with delirious pleasure. Her mother set down the mop and put her fists on her hips. "What on earth is so funny? I really was about to call the cops. Where did you run off to?"

Rachel wiped her eyes. "Mama, if you really want to know, I ran off to marry Horace, but he decided he'd rather marry the best man."

"What? Oh, you poor fool!" cried her mother indignantly. "I knew that man was a . . . well, a you-know. Why couldn't you see that? I ought to have told you." She wobbled slightly on her narrow ankles and sat down abruptly in the rose-upholstered armchair.

"Yes," said Rachel, wiping her eyes. "April Fool! That's me. This is the best April Fool's Day I can ever remember. I think I'll celebrate it always. It'll be my new birthday."

"You *were* kidnapped, then," said her mother, panting in her chair. The steam heat was running full tilt. "He kidnapped you and then abandoned you at the altar. It's a wonder you weren't hit by a bus coming home in this mess."

"The buses aren't running, Mother. I was fine."

"Well, I think we should sue him for . . . something." Rachel's mother pulled a hanky from her sleeve and fanned herself deliriously.

"Mother, if you don't settle down, you're going to have a stroke," said Rachel sensibly. "Look, you don't need to fix anything. I am perfectly fine. You and the judge can both just, well, shut your mouths."

"What did you say?"

Rachel stood up and folded her classified ads into a tidy square. "Mother, I said you can Just. Shut. Up." She strode to the phone table and picked up the handset.

"Are you calling Horace?" her mother asked. "You'll let me give him a piece of my mind."

"No. I have other plans," said Rachel as she listened to the confident rattle of the dial.

After a checkered career, Grace Morledge has circled back to writing. She lives in Durango, Colorado.

Water Holds Memory

Kendall Dixon Calhoun

My first cast sends ripples across the glassy lake,
Before the sun has even crept over the mountain tops.
With care, I tie the perfect knot
and choose my favorite lure,
A yellow Panther Martin—my grandfather's favorite.
I pick it in his memory.
I sit and wait, feeling for the gentle tug on my line.
But even if it never comes, I could spend all day here,
In solitude, playing a quiet game of chance with the waters,
My toes resting in its cool embrace.

The memory surfaces, clear as the water before me
The day my grandfather took me fishing.
The sky darkened, and soon, the rain began to pour.
We hurried back to the dock,
The urgency in his movements reflected in his furrowed brow

As he tied up the boat with hands that knew the ropes too well.
Worry etched on his face,
He glanced back at me,
No doubt expecting disappointment,
But instead, I turned to the sky,
A smile breaking across my face as I welcomed the rain,
If he only knew—this moment, this rain-soaked memory,
Would become one of my favorites.
In that downpour, I found joy,
In his care, I found love,
And in the rain, I found a memory to hold onto,
As enduring as the waters that ripple before me.

I watch the sun dip below the horizon,
The same way I watched it rise.
If I could choose my perfect day,
I'd return here tomorrow,

In solitude, I leave the quiet lake behind me
With the rain-soaked memory
Of a man who shaped who I've become.
Always calling me back to the water
Where I still find him, where I still find myself.

Kendall is a twenty-nine-year-old banker by day and a closet poet by night. Moving here in elementary school, Kendall has lived in Cortez for eighteen years and is currently raising her children in the community. She has been writing poetry since childhood, using it as a cherished outlet to express herself and explore the memories that have shaped who she is today.

· E S S A Y ·

in the space between

Dai Salwen

The Verde River Valley is wild unlike anywhere else I know. Some might call it the middle of nowhere, the blank space on a map. North of Phoenix, south of Flagstaff, and west of towns whose names rarely leave the lips of travelers, there is a space where wildness convenes.

It is a place where white man's delineation of land gets muddy. The Coconino and Tanto national forests mingle with the Mazatal and Cedar Bench wildernesses all lovingly caressing this one river valley. If you look on a map, you'll find old roads meandering down to the river. Locked gates and boulders the size of wheels tell a different story.

My partner and I come here every year. When the snow drifts are deep in the Colorado mountains, we fill our well-worn hatchback with backpacks and sleeping bags and make our pilgrimage to the neighboring land whose sweet song beckons us to come rest a while in her feral bosom. We trade out road dust for feet on sand and the rough jagged rocks of the valley walls cheekily bid us to enter. This land offers her warm embrace in the form of thorns left under skin. Her kisses are warm sunlight on arms and legs and the breathtaking cold of snowmelt water enveloping bodies. When I see her flesh snaking through the desert soil I exhale, shedding off layers of skin I didn't know I was wearing.

On this particular trip, there is a new locked gate to add to the long list of ways you can't reach the Verde Valley. I can picture each curve of that road, each washboard straightaway and each steep descent, just as every child knows the trees along their path home from school. Down that road and across the river is a sycamore tree on a grassy bank. Her roots sink deep into the sandy soil and her brown leaves twist and dance in the wind. She looks out over a playfully booming rapid whose name brings a delighted smile to my face.

And so, undaunted by metal poles and chains, we set out on a new journey with the sycamore as our guide. We drive hours just to park eight miles upriver, down a road we've never traveled and next to a ranch that rarely sees visitors.

Mind you, eight miles on the Verde River is not like eight miles down a country road. The land pinches, buckles, drops and rises, and sometimes, all your forward progress is met by an impassable fissure dipping deep into the earth or an insurmountable cliff wall looming above you.

Usually, when we travel in the river valley, we take the river corridor knowing that this is the way the wild beings travel and their paths are good ones. As the river snakes through its bed, it bounces off the walls. Often, bends demand that travelers cross the water twice just to reach the next straight away.

When we travel the riverbed we listen for the sound of rapids and look for the sharp bends that dictate that it is time to cross. We often find ourselves hip deep with packs on our backs carefully picking our way through the icy rushing water. When we exit, our skin is red and tingling. In these moments I feel myself come alive, as if I had been walking through life asleep without knowing it. The river always washes something away with it downstream.

On this particular trip, we didn't immediately dip down to the riverbanks the way we usually do. The map told of a trail on the highlands that would reach almost to our destination and so we decided to take a chance.

But just as the roads in this river valley end as unmet expectations, this trail too seemed destined to unravel. We found it and lost it and found it again, weaving farther and farther from the river. We kept telling ourselves that maybe after the next rise, we'd reach some flat on the top of something that would allow us some easy miles downriver. But the easy miles never came. Looking out on the far rolling hills—oh, rolling hills does not describe it; how about *on the jagged mountainous, crevices and peaks*—we realized there was no place for us up here. No easy journey. No respite along this long-forsaken trail.

And so, scratched up by Mesquite and Catclaw with tired ankles from navigating loose rocks, we started our descent down into the valley. Down to the water and the willows. To the otters and the river stones.

Just because we decided to go down, didn't mean that down would be easy. We were traversing land a thousand feet above the water's edge. And so, again we reached a place where easy forward wasn't an option. The rocks crumbled and buckled in front of me. It was time to play our age-old game of, "into mesquite or catclaw?" We knew we'd be offering a small blood sacrifice no matter which plant we chose.

I shimmied my way around the catclaw carefully, pinching a branch and lifting it towards the sky, so that its hooked thorns would leave my skin be. At least, that was the hope. I let my shoulder slowly press against the mesquite, knowing that its thick straight points would be friendly compared to that of its neighbor.

My back was now facing the step down. I swung around and planted one foot and then the other on the earth beneath.

When I turned, I saw a face staring right back at me from the ground next to my foot. Black as a Labrador. Head big as a Pyrenees. I stared, shocked and confused. My brain could not process who this was in front of me. Lost dog? Badger? It was probably less than a second before my mind finally clicked to "bear," but I did not wait around to process this realization. I screamed a blood curdling scream, as I often do for surprises of all shapes and sizes, and scrambled back up through the catclaw with no thought for my skin or clothes or pack. My partner who stood above me chuckled as he often does for my misplaced screams. He looked down to see the baby bear's head poking out of the stone den. Wide eyed, the bear looked left and then right and then left again, presumably searching for the strange creature who had stood at his doorstep and screamed in his face.

Once it was clear that I was no longer standing in wait, he bolted from his hiding place down the ravine and up again, loping full tilt with hands between feet until his black behind dipped around a rock and out of our sight.

I quietly whispered under my breath, "I'm sorry."

"I'm sorry, I yelled at you."

"Thank you for letting us see you."

"Thank you."

As I caught my breath, I chuckled. My heart filled with deep gratitude for this land. For its wildness. For the wild ones. For my life that allows me these moments that I never would even think to ask for. I am so grateful to know that every time I come to these places, I become part of the great mystery of wildness. Here I get to know myself as a brother and a sister in a magnificent family.

And so, with a smile, we left that particular catclaw behind. We wove our way farther along the edge of the ravine before dipping down in a different place so as to give that bear and his cave a large berth.

I wondered if that bear would ever see another human. I wondered if his mother had ever seen a human in this place that seems to disappear from humanity's awareness, as spaces without roads or towns often do.

Within the hour, scratched tired and relieved, our feet step down onto river stones. Sparkling blue water meets us as an inn keeper meets her weary travelers. Legs wet and hearts light, we start our journey again down river.

Dai is an artist, creator, and guide located in Mancos, Colorado. They strongly believe that acknowledgment of and reverence for the wild world is a key part of what it means to be a good human. Their hope is that in some small way the works they create can help us all be a little more connected to the land and the beings that live on it. You can find their art at www.practiceofhonoring.com.

Water Will Find You
(because you belong here)

Renee Podunovich

I. Junctures

All roads end. Especially an unmaintained, 2-track county road in-
creasingly indistinguishable from landscape—an obstacle course of
boulders and ruts that will knock the bottom out of the vehicle un-
less you stop, park, put on your daypack. And begin to trek.

Here, my footprints begin. Stirring fine flushed dust rising in spirals
with each step. Airborne and errant on Spring Equinox winds that
whoosh a primordial oomph. Carrying the smell of minerals and
ancient silt. The touch of saltwater on swaying waves. Hues of ceru-
lean ice melt. Songs of elk bugling under moonlight.

They draft on invisible vapors from snow-covered crests. From as far west as the Pacific Ocean and its volatile fault lines holding the visions dreamed by sunsets.

II. Anonymous

On some spring days in the high desert, the wind is intolerable. But today, it feels like being shaken awake, purified, cleansed. My hair and lungs full of disorderly elemental intersections. I am in a new current. I accept this baptism by whirlwind, this walk into expanses so endless it is like stargazing. Snow from distant mountain ranges travels beside me, though its path is elusive in this bone-dry vastness, and that moisture is never easy to discover. Through Sage, Juniper and Yucca tangled into a weaving of peculiar geological mishaps, I travel so far that I am suddenly small and unknown. But somehow at home.

How awe is simply the sudden recognition of place—a sense of belonging to the vastness you had forgotten.

III. Desert Emeralds

Hidden by boundlessness—sudden chasms. At the edge of one of hundreds of crisscrossing canyons, I can see a pool of water lingering in the bottom, evidence of a recent snowstorm. Sparkling a promise of well-being, it beckons me down a narrow path.

Suddenly, cold, damp air rises from a sandstone overhang, greets my dusty face, shivers my mammalian body, invites me into a shallow cave with walls covered by vibrant, verdant moss, green like a supernova, feeding on snowmelt seeped through underground stone shelves. Droplets hit small pools of transparent water—*rippling, rippling, rippling*.

IV. Here You Are

There is no other sound than water meeting water. Of my breath caught in eternity. No other moment, no other reason needed to open my heart again. Despite impending endings, some jewels emerge in unlikely places; create a motivation to keep traveling bumpy side roads, to keep going no matter how and despite obstructions.

There will be moments like this. Don't despair any longer.

Water will find you.

Renee Podunovich is a poet, printmaker, photographer, and collage artist. She focuses on cyanotype and alternative printing processes and analog and digital collages. Her work has been featured in regional exhibits such as "Satchel Story Objects" a collaborative exhibit funded by The National Endowment for the Arts through Colorado Creative Industries. Her cyanotypes have been featured in online photography spaces, including Analog Forever Magazine's Top 40 Analog Photographs of 2023.

Renee has three chapbooks of poems: Illustrious for Brief Moments *(Finishing Line Press, 2021),* Let the Scaffolding Collapse *(Finalist of the New Women's Voices Chapbook Competition by Finishing Line Press, 2012), and* If There Is a Center No One Knows Where It Begins *(Art Juice Press, 2008). She is the 2019 Cantor Award winner awarded by the Telluride Literary Festival.*

Fifi

Aidan Gaughran

When I was younger, everyone told me I would be snatched up by a witch. The abduction would happen at nighttime, or at the precise moment I strayed off alone, away from human eyes. *"Te va a llevar la turivieja."* The witch is going to get you. My mother, my brothers, my *abuelos*, cousins, aunts and uncles, children younger than me, and, yes, even complete strangers have all told me this on multiple, separate occasions. The words slide off the tongue with great ease and no qualms. After the words come wide eyes and a taut face, and then a tense silence – apparently the witch is so bad that she needs no further explanation.

We burn, poison, and maim these hills, and in return they give us our food and our homes. These are plain facts. What is less plain, yet no less significant, is how the hills affect us beyond their fertility. They loom large, waiting to spill onto us, enclosing us in a chamber. And in this chamber, I have come to find that the same small number of stories echo and bounce around before settling like an evening mist, blanketing out all difference and creating for the people an invisible pact so that we can sleep comfortably with the angels at night.

Along with the witch there are the mischievous dwarves, the sinister snakes, and almighty God. I have spent many moons with the first two – when the moon is new, the dwarves and I tie knots in the manes of horses as they sleep; the snakes and I weave tree branches into crawling routes on high – and can confirm that they (we) are relatively harmless co-conspirators of the witch. The general rationale of the people in my village seems to be to avoid the witch, the dwarves, and the snakes at all costs, while immersing oneself completely, utterly, within God. There is no middle ground. It's not that I don't believe in these stories. God is good, witch is bad. I just don't believe in the people that tell them.

The story my mother and everyone else tell about the *turivieja* goes something like this: she sleeps by day and comes out at dusk, looking for the child she had and lost some time ago. She can be anywhere, sometimes in two places at once, but she especially lurks among the dark winding riverbanks. No one knows what she looks like, at least no one who's still alive. Her presence is heard and felt, but not seen. One thing for certain is that she lets out a scream that mimics that of a distressed infant, either out of insane grief or in the hope she'll receive one in return. What happens to he or she who encounters the *turivieja* depends on the whim of her emotions (a topic I will address later.)

Last Saturday, my uncle Eliseo was stumbling back from a *baile* when he heard her scream, and he's been bedridden, ears ringing, ever since. Seven and a half years ago my cousin went to the swimming hole *solito* and the *turivieja* swallowed him whole. Only his sandals remained on the rocky outcrop from which he jumped, unknowingly, to his death.

These are the stories I and every young child hear growing up in my village. But hearsay (what people here say) is one thing, and reality is another, and I have reached the age where I feel the need to distinguish between the two. I already said that I have spent many moons with the dwarves and the snakes. But I have spent the most moons with the "witch," whom I will henceforth call Fifi. I feel strange calling her a witch, because to me, she has always just been Fifi. What follows is the fruit of my encounters with her.

In this lifetime I will not forget my first brush with Fifi because that was the night my heart started beating to the tune of something beyond me. My mom had fallen asleep, as she always does, to whatever *telenovela* was playing on Channel 12. I slipped from her clutches, placing a pillow in my stead. The volume on the TV was barely audible, and I remember wondering if it would be enough to cover up my thumping chest. I took a deep breath and lifted the chair (which weighed more than a dead horse), brought it to the opposite wall, and crawled through the window into the night. This was a month after Miguel had drowned; I was nine. I found my feet and whispered to myself, *tonight I will meet the turivieja.*

The darkness was heavy, the air neither warm nor cool. A gentle breeze – my momentum against the night – tickled the ears as I slithered down the hill behind our house, under the fence, past the pasture. A sole rooster crooned, marking the hour. Up above, the moon was playing hide and seek with the clouds. Past the coffee trees, leaves trembled side to side. In the absence of light I used my toes as antennas, probing the roots and the divots. Past the tall, straight pine, Abuela's voice sang in my head, "God made the day for the people and the animals to buzz, fly, amble about. And He picked everyone up at night, to rest."

A series of hoots and shrieks rose from a nearby ravine, and I headed in that direction. The river hummed in the distance, drunk from all the day's rain. Somewhere between the pine and the ravine it occurred to me that I had never felt so alone. The horror of feeling lost boiled inside me and crept up to the bottom of my throat. I wanted my mother, and to be cloaked in the familiar. I closed my eyes, wept, and had the strange sensation of some force pulling me against my own will. My ears started ringing, and the hum of the river grew louder.

I have never told anyone in my village what happened next, because I would rather avoid the drama of having the Devil exorcised from me when it was never there in the first place. But I will tell you. You might think I'm weird, but so be it.

The hum grew so loud that I forgot my fear of being lost. I forgot my mom, and I forgot my nine-year-old self. I was weightless, I was nothing. And then I found myself in the middle of what can only be described as an insect bonanza. Cicadas whined overhead. Beetles lined the bark of trees. Crickets beep-beep-beep-beeped. Phosphorescent moths draped mossy rocks on the riverbank, and giant grasshoppers hopped on their backs. And there we were, Fifi and I, darting silently to and fro, catching anything I could get my hands on and that she could get her beak on.

After we'd grown full, Fifi and I flew so that my bellybutton skimmed the river's surface. I drank from the gushing water, suspended in the air. I grew tired, I dozed off. When my mother woke me in the morning, she told me to bathe and get dressed for school. The window was closed, and the chair was back in its place.

Everyone here seems to agree that Fifi is a "witch" that makes a weird infant-like noise down by the river, which qualifies her as something to be feared. This reduction is the mist that descends on the people, and the mist is why no one has ever really *seen* Fifi. They hear a sound, intuit a presence, feel discomfort, and they conflate these three disparate things into the *turivieja*. The mist blots out the subtle details, which are the most crucial.

First and foremost, Fifi is a shapeshifter. So while hawk is hawk, mouse is mouse, and you are you, Fifi is never any of these, at least for longer than a day. You may be wondering how I know Fifi is Fifi, and not just any other animal or human. The answer is that I don't; I can only assume. I like to think she reveals herself when she pleases. Once, while clearing brush, she met me as a hummingbird. We froze face to face. She cocked her head to one side, gave me the up-down, and said, "Huh, I thought you were a flower" before buzzing away. It strikes me that, probably most of the time, I am unaware of her presence. A wave of panic runs through me after I kill a fly or a chicken, because what if it was Fifi?

Since Fifi is always changing, so is our relationship. Each is never totally certain of the other. She is not taken with me, at least not always. Fifi, like most humans, is capable of the very good, and she is capable of the very bad. Like most animals, she is subject to instinct and urges. And like both animals and humans, she is at the mercy of strange dreams and fears beyond her control. (I once awoke in her web. Her sticky spider legs spun me round and round, which she later admitted doing so that I might "see what it's like to wait to die.") We have come to appreciate the times when we truly see each other, whoever we are, in that particular moment.

A few years back, when I was fifteen, we shared one of these amicable encounters where the water was flat and meandered like an S, at the oxbow downriver from where we first met. The moon waned and threw slender shadows that spilled off the trees and onto the water's surface. I lay on my back on a fallen log, looking up into the night canopy. I stole glances at Fifi, who was in her middle human years, with a button nose and a round face not unlike my Tía María. Her pink candy-cane dress (in her words, her "Sunday best") followed her as she drifted, knee deep, between moonlight and shadow, shadow and moonlight, stabbing shrimp with her long fingernails. I was nervous. It was more than six years since we first had met, and though I'd accumulated a vast skill set of aviation, underwater breathing, night vision, and parental disobedience, I knew very little of her personal life, or lives.

So I just blurted out, "Fifi?"

"Ahoo?" She didn't look up.

"Why me?"

She stopped wading, her dress bunching around her knees. She squinted at me and said, "How do you mean?"

"That night, the ears ringing, the insects, the water."

"Are you asking why I picked you up that night?"

"Yes."

She snorted, and continued wading. "All of my prey was right there for the taking. I wanted your help harvesting."

I kept prodding. "But why are we here now, you and me? Why am I the only one that knows you as Fifi, and not as some deranged witch?"

She was surprised at my curiosity, my insistence. Her shoulders sank as she looked at, or through, the moonlit surface.

"Everyone's always running away from me. That night, you were looking for me. And it felt good."

She continued, "Maybe you'll understand this when you're older. But before, before even your *abuelos*, people distinguished between the beings of the night. They knew of us, talked with us, treated us with respect.

"And then things changed. First came the road, then the Church, and then the lights, and people here forgot what it felt like to be lost. So when they heard the tree frogs chirping, the cicadas buzzing, the night hawk singing, they thought it was one thing. They thought it was me."

It occurred to me at that moment that I looked like one of my many neighbors that spend the Sunday sermons staring at the priest in a sort of stupor.

"And doesn't that bother you? That they forget? That they think you're something you're not? It bothers me. To me, you're normal."

"Ha!" She plopped down on a rock, a shrimp longer than an ear of corn squirming at the end of her fingernail. She plucked the claws, snapped where tail met body, and shucked the exoskeleton, all in one swift motion. She produced a lemon, dressed the shrimp, and dropped it in her mouth. She did not finish chewing before continuing, "I've found I have little control over what people think." She swallowed, stuck her face in the river and took a big gulp. "I have myself to worry about, whoever that is."

Her gaze drifted up and found the moon. She then asked, "You know what really bothers me?"

"What?"

"I'm always leaving, shedding whatever I thought was mine at a particular point in time. Waking up and, from the very beginning, feeling a loss that I can't see, but that I must find and fill in. There is an image, a dream that comes back to me every time I wake up like this," she said, looking down at her soaked dress and long fingernails.

"I am swimming upstream, under water, towards the swimming hole when I feel the kerplunk of a splash up ahead. I don't know why I'm going, but I know I must get there. Schools of minnow scatter as I make my way through the muck, sliding past slimy rocks. Two thin legs come into view, kicking to stay afloat. I peck them, and they kick harder. My nose breaks the surface, and I wait for his eyes to find me. He is a boy no more than 12 years old. He finds me. He has doe-like eyes; big, dark almonds. He is beautiful. And he looks at me and says, 'Mama?' And a surge of panic runs up my spine, for I don't know this boy, but he seems vaguely familiar. What if he is mine, and I am forgetting?

"'Is that you?' I ask.

"I can't speak. I feel weak, like I am being pulled away, downriver, from where I came. I want to stay in this moment, grab hold of this boy and wrap myself in him and he in me. To fall to the bottom of the hole and hide in some nook where the current won't reach. And just before I am about to pull him to me, I wake up."

Fifi's eyes peered past the depths of the water and into the earth itself. She muttered, to no one in particular, "He's not real. None of it is real."

I shuddered. I knew no words to comfort myself or Fifi. All was quiet save for the beings of the night. I don't know how long we held the silence before two *muchachos*, riding after a day of heavy drinking and rice cutting, broke it downriver. They rode in tandem, and as they crossed the river they shouted to each other: "*Auuoo-wey! Auuoo-wey! Auuoo-wey! Ah! Oh! Ah! Oh! Ah! Oo-wey!*"

Fifi rose from her rock and gave a cry that sounded like an owl, a frog, a cat, and a child all at once: "*Yip yip yip! Rawwrrmyeehaw! Ti-ti-coo-coo, ti-ti-coo-coo!*" My ears started buzzing again.

Fifi laughed to herself, turned to me, and asked, "Is that what the *turivieja* sounds like?"

Downriver, a whip cracked the stale air, and hurried hooves scuttled into the night.

Aidan Gaughran has called the Four Corners home for three years. In the seven years prior, he lived in various places abroad, where he learned to listen and marvel at the thin line that exists between the magic and the real.

the i that grows unseen in the desert

Kirbie Bennett

angelthreads of green with sunflower dots
are waving through
        red earth in midsummer
beneath a sun-faded heaven slumbering in the sky

the seeds return to the soil
& there is a shadow hiding behind my mouth
begging me for the sound of defeat
& black mold colonizes my insides
asking if i am giving nazi salutes in my sleep

sometimes in dreams i am reborn
with earthprayer

the seeds return to the soil
& there is a shadow behind the phantom limbs

i carry in my skull
so i shape the dream into a bundle
& i boil water & i feel the heat on my unraveling skin

this is where i bring water to the green music
waiting in a cup:

the seeds return to the soil
when the awe of heat showers herbs, the grassy scent
transports me to the undamaged years:
i'm a child sitting with great-grandma in her house,
          there are cats and crossword puzzles and the calling kettle
(it's a room in my heart that i never leave)

teacups full of days in the everlasting arms of naakidi nánálí
teacups full of wisdom i'm still trying to recover

beneath a sun-faded heaven slumbering in the sky
i bring medicine to my mouth,
flood death with life,
i put teeth to a language,
i put tongue to a name:
the seeds return to the soil

Kirbie Bennett is a writer and audio producer from the Southwest. His print and audio work has appeared in High Country News, KSUT Public Radio, The Durango Telegraph and 68-to-oh5, an online music journal. Kirbie is a member of the Navajo Nation and Durango, Colorado is another place he calls home.

The Truth I Cannot Tell

Kathryn Wilder

After parking the tractor and feed wagon under cover, we walk down from the upper barn, my son Ken with his long strides and quicker pace increasing the distance between us with each step. I see Solstice next to a juniper tree in the house pasture—she's one of my Criollo first-calf heifers, her markings like white clouds in a dark sky. Slowing but not stopping, I note that she just stands, still, away from the other heifers who wait near a gate to be fed.

Snow crunches to ice beneath my Neoprene-insulated, knee-high boots; it measures a foot deep on top of a base layer of packed ice. I'd follow in Ken's footsteps in the fresh snow but they are too far apart. He didn't pause as he passed Solstice.

When we fed the cows in the lower pasture, me driving the tractor, pulling the wagon, Ken balancing back there forking off flakes from a three-quarter-ton hay bale, and piles of cornstalks that give the calves dry places to lie, two new calves bawled forlornly, wet-shivering, ice cubes hanging from their ears. I'm shivering now, the wet snow melting through my knit hat and heavy jacket and insulated overalls into my flannel shirt and silk baselayer and cotton tank top and sports bra, clear to my flesh, where snowmelt meets sweat as I hurry to catch up with Ken. At first I don't notice that his tracks veer off to his house, and when I do I keep hustling toward the hay to get the heifers fed so we can return to the lower pasture where we left the two unclaimed calves bawling miserably.

We saw one of the suspect mothers—206, a tall black-white-face Angus cross—kick at a little bull calf. Black markings like hands coming together in prayer across his white face, he tried and failed to get a teat in his hungry mouth before the cow wandered off. Another cow, a large Black Angus, meandered through the feeding cattle, looking, sniffing, searching for her own newborn. But the second bawling calf, a solid black heifer at the lower end of the field, went unheard by the cow.

I shove pitchfork loads of grass hay over the fence to the heifers. The snow keeps coming. Winter surprises me every year—the cold and the snow—because I grew up coastal and tropical and didn't know until first moving to the desert years ago that deserts are so much more than hot. Ken comes down with a bottle, this for a twin born two weeks ago. The mother took the smaller twin, abandoning Chloe, so named by my granddaughter, to a future as a bottle calf, comfort coming from the grandkids, their mother, and me as we feed her and pet her but we don't lick and low as a mother-cow would, and Chloe is lonely. She butts Ken as he feeds her the bottle. The snow does not cease falling.

"Solstice is standing off by herself," I tell Ken.

"She's fine," he says, finishing with Chloe. "Get the old towels," and he hurries past me, back up to his house. I go to mine, not bothering to remove anything wet from my body, chunks of snow tracking me across the cement floor. The stack of towels stands ready on the couch, laundered and stiff from air-drying by fireplace-insert heat. The dryer doesn't work. Something about the 220-power source. We have to dig down to the powerline with the backhoe when the earth thaws. This winter my life hangs by the fire.

Ken has my old Toyota Tacoma running, exhaust fuming behind it. Towels thrown on the backseat, a fresh bottle between my feet, the heater turned up high, "Solstice," I say.

Ken gasses through the ruts left by the morning feeding, snowdrifts already filling the furrows. "I saw her with another heifer. She's fine. We have to see what's going on down here."

I jump out to open the gate, snow slapping my face, and leave the gate open as the cows won't venture out while there's still hay on the ground. On the snow. Ken maneuvers across the snowfield through humps of calves mouthing hay or lying on cornstalk beds. Cows munch with their heads down, or up as they eye us, wondering if we're here to feed them again already. There's the tiny prayer-faced bull calf, his voice loud and mournful despite his shivering. And the heifer, farther away, her cry wrenching through the hush of snow. As the tall cow, 206, heads off toward shielding trees, we follow her. She stands in the snow-shadow of a large, thick-branched one-seed juniper, looking around, confused. She half-circles it, sniffing the snow and the branches and the detritus near the trunk, and walks back toward the hay.

"She's too old to be stupid," Ken says, which means that first-calf heifers can be like I was when I had Ken, not knowing exactly how to nurse or clean my baby, while to seasoned mothers those acts come easily, and cows can usually find their calves. But in this cold, wet-snow morning something has happened that threw the cow—and us—off.

In the blizzard of snow and cows feeding we don't see the second cow, but there's the prayer calf bawling to the sky. Ken drives close, stops, throws open the door and grabs the calf and I open the back door and he tosses the calf onto the seat. Twisting awkwardly, I get a towel and start rubbing. "Not too much," Ken says. "Leave some mother's scent on him."

Ken has the bottle. Inside the Toyota's heat I start to sweat but the calf trembles with cold as I rub him and break ice cubes off his ears. Ken inserts the nipple and pulls it when the calf's lips find it and soon the calf latches on, drinking with deep gulps, and Ken takes the bottle away. As I keep the calf from climbing onto the console between us Ken drives the small truck toward 206, who looks across the white landscape, the air so thick with white I can't see the promontories and ridges of the Mesa Verde skyline, or even the piñon-juniper rim of this pasture.

Ken pulls close, steps out, grabs the calf from the backseat and sets it near 206, who we hope really is its mother. Invigorated but not full from the warm milk in his belly, the prayer calf reaches for the teat, the cow turns away, and he follows; she stops, he butts her, she lets him suck, and we head toward the next calf. The second possible new-mother cow stops at a white lump on the ground, sniffs through the cold cloak of snow, and the calf jumps up and goes right to nursing, still hump-backed, legs curved from the womb.

"Also born today," I say, noting the cow's ear tag number to record later. Storms bring on the calves. Six calves will be born this day. Ken and I won't stop working until well after dark.

The little all-black heifer has increased her piteous wailing. Ken plows through the snow toward her and we repeat the abduction-and-warming process. When we plop her back in the snow, no one pays attention. Then through the blurring white we see 206, head up, looking, sniffing the cold air even as the prayer calf nurses.

"Shit," Ken says.

"Twins?"

"We don't need more twins," he says. But he steps out and grabs the black heifer again, thrusting her onto my lap, and steers to 206.

I push out of the passenger seat with the calf in my arms and run three steps toward the cow, set the calf down, and jump back into the Toyota before the cow can give chase, which they're wont to do. Ken backs up twenty feet and we watch. The prayer calf still latched on, the tall cow sniffs this new being; she sniffs through towel and people smells to her own scent and starts licking the cold away.

"Yep, twins." I take off my sopped hat, my hair also wet. Hats and gloves on the dash near the heater vents we leave the pasture, close the gate, and park near the barn.

"Let's get dry before checking them again," Ken says.

I'm already through the gate into the house pasture where the first-calf heifers eat hay in the snow. Solstice is with them. I walk among them, looking at bags and vulvas, which tell me how close they are to calving. "Solstice's bag is huge," I say to Ken's back.

He's heading toward his house. "I saw her earlier. She's fine."

I look. Some blood on her tail. Her vulva smaller than yesterday. Her bag tight. "She's calved. I'm going to look for her calf." I walk north through the snow toward where Solstice stood alone under the juniper, not noticing that Ken has climbed the fence and headed west. I see only lumps of cowshit covered in snow—any one of them could be a tiny calf—and I trip toward one then another then to the spot by the juniper and it's lying there stone still, red fur wet from snow and birth-slick and I fall to my knees, shedding my gloves and feeling it for heat for breath for life and with none of that present I pick up its head and try to make it breathe as I cry out like the twins in the lower pasture bawling to the sky.

I shake it. Cold. Nose mouth ears cold. Ken walking toward me along the fenceline. "Is it alive?" he says. I thought he'd gone inside.

I shake my head. Shake my heart. I shake the calf—truly there's no life in there. The afterbirth pooled nearby. When I saw Solstice earlier, alone beside the tree, I walked past without stopping to look more closely. Without climbing the fence into the pasture to check on my first-calf heifer who was born on winter solstice high on a plateau among junipers and piñon pines in an 11,000-acre pasture to a cow we had bought without knowing she would calve out of season and I hadn't watched closely, only noticed that she went missing in a snowstorm and I looked for her then, combing through hills and trees for two days until I found not only the pair but the birthplace. I named the cow Walkabout, the calf Solstice, and today I walked past Solstice without stopping to check her and I can tell you I hated myself right then.

Ken tells me to go get warm, and heads to his house. He feels terrible, too, I know.

I stay kneeling in the snow before the calf, both of us wet to the skin. Solstice had not finished cleaning her off. Yes, her. A tiny red heifer. Full Criollo. For what reason did she die. All I can think is I was not there.

I've only done it once, though I have wanted to many times. When I got clean—went through detox and five weeks of inpatient treatment and no longer had drugs to use when the white lightning of pain or anger seared through me—my mind went to cutting, to hurting me bigger than whatever caused the hurt. It felt good, this truth I have not told, my sharp hunting knife slicing through the skin of my arm—that part where other people get banded tattoos— slicing again and again until the outer skin split like when you skin an animal and the elastic of the hide separates to reveal flesh and the blood slowly seeps to the surface and beads. I walk away from the tiny calf to check on her mother, thinking about where to cut. How deep. I'm burning.

Solstice is eating. Which of my knives is sharp enough, I wonder. Inside beside the fire I pull layers of clothing like skin off my body. Jacket heavy with snowmelt, draped over a chair, dripping, the straps of the insulated overalls pulled off my shoulders, hanging from my waist. The calf lying dead in the snow. The wrists? Flannel shirt shed. Another log on the fire, sparks flaring. My hair dripping down my back through black silk baselayer and cotton tank and bra. Calf dead. *Dead!* Because I didn't stop, instead hurrying after someone else's agenda. My skin red with cold as I peel off silk. Heat reaching me finally from outside, fire still burning within—in my stomach, my arms. White lightning I called it when rage burned down my arms and I wanted to strike out but now I want to strike in again and again and I look at the crinkled skin of my past on arms where sun has burned and points have punctured, there, I look for the tracks of old pain. From before. Before I got clean. The before and after of me. Young and old, the same and different, unidentical twins, both me, all me; Ken at the door. Entering.

"We better go check on them." He steps back outside.

Still in my boots, having not pulled them or overalls off, I find dry silk and flannel and cover my skin and scars and pull the overalls up, straps over my shoulders, the jacket on, and a dry hat.

Toyota already running, warm, "I looked at Solstice's calf," Ken says. "Its hooves are clean. No mud or dirt from trying to stand. It never got up."

"It's snowing. The hooves wouldn't show dirt."

"It was either stillborn or suffocated from the sack over its nose."

"I didn't stop. *I didn't stop.* I was following you. *You* didn't stop."

"I didn't see her." He hadn't looked sideways. The big hood of his jacket like blinders. He didn't see her.

"I told you she was standing, alone."

He drives through more drifting snow. "I saw her earlier, with other heifers."

"But I *told* you. You didn't listen." The fight is in me and I want it out.

"*You* didn't listen," he says, "to your own intuition. *My* intuition told me to get to these two calves. Yours was telling you to stop, go look. But if she was just standing still, the calf was already dead. She'd already had it and it was dead."

He stops at the gate. I get out, want to slam the door, prop the gate open on snow, get back in, and Ken drives toward the cattle. We scan the cows—there's 206, foraging through what's left of the hay. She hasn't slipped her afterbirth; the string of it hangs beneath her tail. Most of the calves huddle on piles of hay or cornstalks. I see the small curl of the prayer calf like a dog sleeping, but the black heifer stands, bawling.

I look at Ken. "Would Solstice take it?"

"You mean graft it on her?"

"We could try."

He watches 206, an older cow. She looks worn out. Confused by the twins but trying to make it right. Afterbirth hanging, which happens—they don't always pass it cleanly like Solstice did—but sometimes it represents problems.

Ken maneuvers toward the bawling black heifer. "We better do it now before the cow gets attached," and he's out the door and the calf's in the back and we slip and slide away before 206 knows what's missing, stopping for the gate and again at the barn, where Ken puts the new calf with bottle-calf Chloe temporarily and I trudge through the snow to get the little dead heifer, holding her snugly to my chest like my own newborns.

Ken has a large box cut open and flattened on the cement floor of the barn. I lie the heifer down on the cardboard bed, my hand resting on her forehead for only a moment. Ken looks at her. His hunting knife sharp, ready, he rolls the calf onto her back, exposing the belly. Knife near the throat, he slices into the skin, following the line down to her navel, sometimes going over a spot again and again until the outer skin splits and the inner flesh is revealed, red as the little heifer's coat, which the black heifer will soon wear.

I watch my son on his knees on the cold floor, both of us cold and tired though it's still morning—tired of the year, the drought despite snow, death; he concentrates, careful with the sharp knife, following a pattern his father taught him, a pattern hunters know, but he deviates, the calf not gutted like a deer, stripped only, the hide sliced cleanly around the wrists, but they're ankles, really, so the black heifer's legs will go through like arms into sleeves.

I step back out into snowflakes and bring Solstice into a pen. Ken has finished skinning. The naked carcass stays on cardboard and he dresses the black heifer, pushing her front hooves through the sleeves of the dead calf's hide, which stretches over her back, then pushing the hind feet through. It must be cold to the live heifer at first, certainly strange. We have to hurry to get her warm. As Ken readies the squeeze chute I move Solstice from one pen to another, pressing her forward with my voice, my body near her ribs, her hip, and she enters the chute and Ken closes the gate behind her and squeezes her slightly with a lever above his head. She's caught and stands quietly but he puts a cow halter on her anyway, dallies the lead rope around a bar, hands me the end of the rope, and I hold her head so she can't fight as he maneuvers the black heifer in her new red coat toward a teat. Solstice kicks at first but Ken's persistence helps the calf find the teat and warm milk dribbles down her throat and it's good and she suckles for more.

Kathryn Wilder, author of the Colorado Book Award-winning Desert Chrome: Water, a Woman, and Wild Horses in the West, *lives in Disappointment Valley and Dolores, Colorado. A longer version of "The Truth I Cannot Tell" will be included as a chapter in* The Last Cows, *forthcoming from Bison Books in 2025. This piece was also previously published in the literary journal, Fugue (Fall, 2021).*

On The Road to Julius' Sheep Camp

Christy Ferrato

The earth turns red,
clouds percolate, and crows scatter,
chunks of meat dangling from their mouths.
They fly over tumbleweeds and salt cedar,
from Nenahnezad to Burnham,
searching for wishbones and grace notes.

Snaking through the desert brush
and dry creek beds, yellow helmeted workers
blast and check iron claws that harvest coal.
Narrow ruts lead to Julius' shack.
Rumbling ground scares sheep, and he
has left to search for his lost flock.

A skinny stray barks at my arrival because
I smell like the trespassers who have come

to drill and strip mine. He keeps his distance,
ribs showing.

A bloated cow lies on the side of the road,
hooves pointing to the sky.

Christy Ferrato's work has been featured in lectures, publications, poetry performances, and exhibitions including the Lake Eden Arts Festival, the Taos Poetry Festival, the Re(dress) Poetry series in Los Angeles, the Fort Collins Museum of Contemporary Art, the Durango Arts Center, the Henderson Fine Arts Center, the Ray Drew Gallery, and the Vermont College of Fine Arts. Poet, artist, educator, and performances artist, Christy explores the intersection of poetry with other art forms to consider how we might transcend our stained histories. Questions about social justice are integral to work that is responsive to historical omission and erasure, and gives voice to what has been lost in the shadows of silence.

Back When Koby Knew Luke

Danielle Emerson

Koby's childhood best friend was a tall, scrawny Navajo boy named Luke. He was one of those kids who lived outside the rez, on a farm that hadn't seen rainwater since both were children. Their community was in drought and had been since the late nineties. During the summers, they spent a lot of time at an old shack just south of Luke's family farm, a vast expanse of dirt set among acres of cornfields and melons. When Luke lost his grandmother, dying from a long life well lived, their farm slowly went extinct. No one planted anything on the land, choosing instead to fight over the home lease. When Luke talked about it with Koby, he was neither angry nor spiteful.

"I just miss planting," he said, keeping his hands occupied picking weeds by his feet, small rocks between his thumb and pointer finger.

Koby sat next to him on the ditch bank. He didn't really understand what was happening with Luke's family, but what he did know was that Luke wanted things to go back to how they once were. Years later, Koby would wonder if Luke's family ever had a "normal," and if his grandmother's death was simply the match that set everything on fire. This thought made Koby self-conscious; he knew Luke cared a lot about his grandmother, so referring to her as an "incident," and implying that his family was always kind of messed up, well, let's just say he wouldn't take it easily.

"We can plant something," Koby offered, already thinking about all the kinds of vegetable seeds they could scrounge together.

Luke's frown deepened. He wasn't looking at Koby. "It's not the same."

After that, Luke stopped coming over to Koby's house.

Koby thought a lot about the time before Luke's grandmother died. They liked to catch lizards back then, chasing their tails and scooping up their gritty, brown bodies in wide, practiced arcs. When the farm was thriving, dozens of lizards snuck between corn stalks and squash vines. They took turns staring at the lizards' beady eyes, the size of apple seeds, reflecting back a couple of *chizhí* sunburnt faces. Luke would threaten to swallow the lizards whole, sticking out a Red Hot Cheeto-stained tongue and leaning his head back. And, every time, Koby liked to triple-dare him to do it.

"Do it and I'll give you a dollar!"

But Luke never did it. Instead, he threw the lizard at Koby, aiming for his face, and took off running down the dirt road connecting both of their trailers. Koby had mastered dodging, anticipating the toss, and watched as the lizard fell onto its side before scuttling beneath a couple of nearby rocks. In the back of his mind, Koby thought about his grandfather's warnings, *don't be out there catching lizards, they'll peel back your morality.*

Now, Koby was a good kid, so his grandfather wasn't really worried about him, and neither was Koby.

It wasn't until Luke started to pick apart the lizards' limbs that

Koby started to feel uneasy. His father's pocketknife in hand, Luke sliced off the lizard's feet with focused precision. He wasn't messy. It was almost clinical. Koby watched as Luke's hand remained perfectly aligned with the lizard's spine, gliding the dirty blade down to the lizard's stomach, and towards the end of its tail. Koby was always amazed at how easily a lizard's body could be cut open, falling apart like warm butter in Luke's dirt-stained hands. Their bones were thin, smaller than toothpicks, and their intestines fit on the head of a quarter. But Luke didn't care about the bones or the intestines. He wanted the skin.

In fifth grade, Koby didn't think much of Luke's, for lack of a better word, inhumane interests. He just thought that Luke, like Koby, wanted to be a doctor. On the playground, or behind a small cluster of Joshua trees out on Luke's farm, Koby sat back and watched as his childhood friend tore apart lizard after lizard, discarding everything but the small, rough stretch of skin. It almost seemed like Luke was trying to make a lizard coat, the kind that fell by your ankles and draped heavy sleeves over your arms. Koby wondered if Luke's fascination with lizard skin would be enough.

An older teacher caught Luke with a dead lizard in his pocket once and made him stay after school. Luke wailed and begged to keep the lizard, but the teacher simply dropped it in the trash, a soft thud that meshed with the plastic trash bag. Koby walked home from school that day alone. Right as he stepped onto the dirt road, in the corner of his eyes, he caught a flicker of movement. He turned his head, and a pair of small black dots met his. Without thinking, Koby followed the lizard into the bushes, dropping to his knees, hands out in front, eyes drawn toward any sign of scurrying. A bit of dirt flew up on his right, and Koby leaped, snatching the lizard in the cup of his hands. He stood up, using his elbows as leverage against the dirt floor, and pressed his thumb and pointer finger against the lizard's stomach, holding the creature in place. It squirmed relentlessly, limbs becoming loose paper in the high desert winds.

Staring at the lizard, Koby took his left pointer finger and ran it across the lizard's head. It felt like an old cat's tongue, a short strip of uneven sandpaper that clung to his skin. He lifted one of the lizard's feet, testing its weight on his fingers, and considered the obvious. All he had to do was pull. And it wasn't like he had to pull that hard; a light tug might be enough to tear its skin.

Koby didn't have a pocketknife, but he had watched Luke dismember lizards hundreds of times; surely, it wasn't as hard as it looked. But the longer Koby stared at the lizard, the more he felt the heat of the lizard's gaze on his face, turning his black hair hot to the touch.

Koby dropped the lizard. It fell between his feet and a terrible part of Koby, a part that seemed far crueler than Luke, urged him to stomp on it. But before he could move, the lizard flipped onto its stomach and slipped behind a wall of dry weeds and disappeared.

On Koby's walk back home, the hot sand burned through his hand-me-down sneakers.

The night before Koby's freshman year of high school, Luke disappeared, along with a young girl from their old elementary school. Both boys had already begun growing apart. Koby showed more interest in school, and Luke spent more time by himself at his family's old farm grounds. Koby didn't think much of Luke's disappearance; for a while, Luke had been talking about running away, maybe living in that old shack his grandparents had built back in the eighties, where they used to play as young kids. But when Koby was called into the office on his first day of high school, he knew that somehow, somewhere, Luke had taken things too far, and it was more than just running away that was on the tight-lipped police officer's mind.

He learned that Luke had kidnapped the young girl and attempted to cut open her stomach. They found the girl on the side of the highway, unconscious, between Shiprock and Farmington. Her arms and legs were covered in bruises, the type that might never heal, and a large incision, almost the width of a kitchen knife, ran across her lower abdomen. Koby didn't ask how the girl got away. He asked where Luke was now. The officer didn't say anything.

And then it clicked.

"The old shack south of the dead farm."

Luke was placed under arrest. And while Koby eventually graduated and moved away, having been awarded a partial scholarship to the University of New Mexico, and, nearly six years later, a residency in California, the image of Luke, at seven years old, holding a lizard above his mouth, threatening to swallow it, never left Koby's mind.

The girl survived, and her family took the rest of their kids and moved to Colorado. Koby never did learn her name.

Whenever Koby returned home, he thought about Luke, wondering if he'd ever see him again at the west-side Walmart or the local Dairy Queen parking lot, wondering if he still had that old pocketknife, and if the young girl's blood had permanently stained his hands, like hot metal branding. When at last Koby became a doctor with his own practice and a messy office at IHS, he wondered if an old, loose-skinned version of his childhood best friend would show up in the exam room, maybe with a tumor or an ulcer, and Koby, with his own surgical knives and prowess, would have to cut Luke open.

But Koby never saw him again.

Danielle Shandiin Emerson is a Diné writer from Shiprock, New Mexico on the Navajo Nation. Her clans are Tłaashchi'i (Red Cheek People Clan), born for Ta'neezaahnii (Tangled People Clan). She has a B.A. in Education Studies and a B.A. in Literary Arts from Brown University.

Ordinary Things

Danielle Desruisseaux

You carry a lot of ordinary things.
The bag by the door
holds plastic and pens
glasses, receipts.
Maybe a mirror to check your face
Maybe a map to see where you're headed

Maybe a brush to calm that head
Maybe mittens, maybe snacks
Maybe good luck charms
Maybe bus fare, maybe batteries
Maybe an orange
slowly molding

Maybe pink lip gloss
(to be shiny again)

Maybe some poems
(two-by-two, Noah's ark)
Maybe a bear suit
(the forest is dark)
Maybe a childhood
(it will all fit)
Maybe a death wish.

Maybe a Marxist or radical speaker
Maybe a signboard, battered and blue
Maybe a bloodstain of unknown source
Maybe another you bled there yourself
Maybe the branch of an old pine tree
(now only a pencil with toothmarks, well-chewed).

Maybe a spoon
(two people in bed)
Maybe runes
(they turn in your head)
Maybe a pillow that wards off bad dreams
Maybe a blanket that's full of holes
Maybe a child's hand laid on your cheek
Maybe a crow.
Maybe Ukraine.
Maybe some doubt. Maybe some pride.
Maybe the endless ridiculous slide
of this moment:
A sigh a word a fist
(the space between atoms)
a stare, a glimpse
(the space between stars)
Close your eyes.

Maybe memory and dreaming and concepts of time.
Maybe questions and conflicts and that missed ride.
Your pasts and futures, your alternate lives
Take a breath.

Maybe chapstick. Maybe mints.
The keys to the car.
Maybe all of these things
as you walk out the door.

Danielle Desruisseaux has lived in Mancos, Colorado for twenty years. She is continually inspired by the big hearts and creativity of the people here. She is starting to think she may not leave.

Visiting the Ancients:
On Horseback and On Foot in Ute
Mountain Ute Tribal Park

Andrew Gulliford

The basic idea was simple: gather some family and friends, find the best local guide and outfitter and ride into the back country of Ute Mountain Ute Tribal Park to visit 800-year-old cliff dwellings. In the 1890s, from their Alamo Ranch near Mancos, the Wetherill brothers had taken tourists in by horseback to visit remote ruins before the establishment of Mesa Verde National Park in 1906. We wanted to follow their old cowboy trails, ride in their horses' hoofprints, and come into the country the way the pioneers did--upright in the saddle, boots in stirrups, eyes peeled for the dark shapes of tiny windows high under the ledges of sandstone cliffs. We sought a sense of discovery, of seeing remote rooms hundreds of feet above the valley floor, and then we'd tie up our horses and begin to climb.

To explore the old way--on the backs of roans, buckskins and bays, with tents, a camp cook, a few wranglers and even a small buckboard wagon to haul in our packs, sleeping bags, and assorted gear. Stay off the main graveled road in Ute Mountain Tribal

Park and instead follow ancient travel routes down Mancos Canyon along the Mancos River. We had it all planned with our Ute Mountain Ute Tribal Park permit, and Ute Mountain guides lined up. No pavement, no assigned camp sites, no electricity, and no cell phone reception. Sleep among the sagebrush and have campfires. Count the stars in Orion's belt and have cowboy coffee served in Granite ware pots blackened by years of breakfast fires.

We expected a few saddle sores and stiff muscles. We expected to see carefully constructed cliff dwellings deep set in south-facing alcoves, and we did. We found prehistoric corn cobs, hundreds of broken pottery sherds, and collapsed kiva roofs. Historic, hand-carved signatures with 19th century dates etched into room blocks. Ute rock art from the 1930s of cattle, horses, and cowboys. What we didn't expect to find was heavy rain, flash flooding, and a tipped over wagon that severely hurt the hip of the guest who had been on the wagon seat. We wanted an adventure and we got one--with a near medical emergency and a difficult horseback crossing of the swollen Mancos River as we tried to ride home.

Ute Mountain Tribal Park is a one-of-a-kind visitor experience. Tourism is small scale and low impact with vigorous hiking and climbing including the ascent of kiva ladders sixty-feet high. What makes the tribal park special is its isolation and the intimacy that develops among twelve to eighteen people who spend an entire day with an authorized Ute guide learning to identify Ute and Ancestral Puebloan rock art.

One day we followed our Ute guide Marshall Deer straight down "Moki steps" or hand-carved Ancestral Puebloan or Anasazi toe holds. First, he disappeared over a cliff, without ropes, and then one of our party descended. Just when my friend shouted, "I can't do this," the guide placed my buddy's feet in toe holds that he couldn't see and he was quickly down to terra firma. With trepidation, we followed. As we quietly entered Hoot Owl House, with amber afternoon light streaming through a rare grove of aspen trees, our guide explained, "The Utes just leave these things alone. These were ceremonial people and we leave their homes alone. It's the pothunters and archaeologists who take everything."

In the solitude of Mancos Canyon eagles and red-tailed hawks soar upwards on thermals. The personal discovery of remote cliff dwellings arrived at by hiking original trails becomes all the more surreal as afternoon thunderclouds rise high against a darkening blue sky. Sheer sandstone cliffs give way to hidden villages shaded by pines and fir trees that grow tall at the heads of canyons. Because the cliff dwellings are approached on foot, guests feel they are among the first non-natives to see the ruins, as indeed they are.

Visitors stoop low to enter ancient T-shaped doorways and examine rocks and boulders etched with long grooves where Pueblo people straightened their arrow shafts. Visitors marvel at small rooms where smoke from fires blackened ceilings. Tourists see prehistoric firepits with distinctive stone heat shields that both trapped and reflected the wood's warmth.

Along every trail lie scattered pottery sherds. In the middle of the park a huge kiva is collapsed and surrounded by sherds of all sizes and descriptions. Lion House, the largest village on the Main Ruins Tour, includes the remains of a sunken D-shaped kiva. Fingerprints are visible in dried mortar between hand-dressed stones. Door lintels made of wood tied together with yucca fiber still reveal the original Ancestral Puebloan knot. Items found in Mancos Canyon include spools of hand-woven thread, turkey feather cordage, yucca fiber pot rests, pieces of woven mats, stone tools, black-on-gray bowls, hammer stones, and small corn cobs from early Southwestern agriculture.

So we had adventure aplenty. We expected a good time on our expedition and we earned one. What we didn't expect was driving rain, rising creeks and flash floods. We should have known the weather would get bad when on the first night a gust of wind completely toppled the cook tent. A big storm was coming. Getting into Mancos Canyon was easy but leaving on the expedition's fourth day proved to be a true 19th century Western experience when the wagon slid and tipped over on a dangerous corner of an old access road. In pouring rain, we unhitched the team of Belgian horses.

Earlier explorers William Henry Jackson, journalist Ernest Ingersoll, and guide John Moss didn't worry about torrential rain in June 1874. The weather was fine and they had plenty of grass for their horses. They were chasing rumors, tall tales, preposterous stories of ancient cities hidden in cliffs somewhere in southwest Colorado. According to legend, Jackson had become irritable over not finding any cliff houses. The trio camped along the river and towards sunset as Jackson complained again about not finding any ruins, one of the party, perhaps John Moss, looked up at the nearby cliff and said, "You mean a ruin like the one right there, high on the cliff face?"

Yes, there in the last light of day shone Two-Story House, one of the first Southwestern cliff dwellings ever photographed. Jackson was elated. At dawn they started the climb up to the site with his heavy camera and tripod. Jackson would photograph and publish the first images of a Colorado cliff dwelling, though he missed the larger sites found deeper in the side canyons now part of Mesa Verde National Park. On the second day out our group, on horseback, rode towards Two-Story House, dismounted, tied our horses, and with our Ute guide began our own morning ascent. By late that afternoon rain started and by the next morning it cascaded off the cliffs, pooled below the rocks, and rushed down previously dry creek beds. As the rain poured down, we knew we could become trapped in the canyons. The only way out was the way we came in—riding horseback across the Mancos River.

Everything we had with us was tied into the wagon, now on its side. Swollen creek waters continued to rise. One of our party, who had been on the wagon seat, fell hard and now had a painful hip. The skies poured. Thunder boomed. The horses skittered sideways across wet rocks and soft caliche soil. We weren't sure we could lift the wagon much less get across the next creek.

As I slogged around in the brown mud trying to untie ropes that secured the wagon's load I realized the creek was rising an inch every five minutes. Soon the bottoms of my boots were under water. Our cowboy outing had taken an unexpected twist. What had been a lark was now all too serious. The trip started on a Thursday morning with clear skies, fresh horses, dry clothes, and endless enthusiasm to retrace the trails of southwest Colorado's earliest Anglo explorers. But on that September Sunday, soaked and cold despite our rain gear, our historic re-enactment had become an authentic adventure. Our ride out of the tribal park raced the rain. Water ran off the brims of our hats and down our backs. Could we get the wagon upright and moving? How badly hurt was our companion with her injured hip? Could we make it across the raging Mancos River before it rose even higher? Were we at risk of hypothermia?

Our outfitter and horseback hero Anne Rapp, a lean cowgirl with silver hair in twin braids, had found an orange flicker feather and placed it in her hatband. Hopi Indians believe finding flicker feathers along a trail is a sign of good luck. With the wagon overturned, creek waters rising, and nine cold, wet, unseasoned riders on horseback, Rapp knew we'd need all the luck we could get.

We had toured Two-Story House, lunched on Moccasin Mesa, carefully crept down Moki steps to the deep quiet of Hoot Owl House, and on the third day explored Hemenway House.

On one of the narrowest ledges I've ever walked, the sky opened, the canyon fell below, and in between short breaths I knew I was on top of the world standing where few people had been in the last thousand years. Carefully I looked over the edge and with binoculars found our horses tied in the distance. To the north was the boundary of Mesa Verde National Park. Far from Mesa Verde's paved tour stops and away from the tribal park's graveled road, our little group was in one of the most remote and inaccessible places in the Four Corners. I took a deeper breath, exulting in our isolation.

When it was time to go, I slipped. I began to fall down the inside of a 25-foot rock chimney I had climbed up. Instantly, Ute guide Roger Wing reached out and caught me in the climber's clasp, forearm to forearm. I left some blood on the rocks, but that was a small price to pay for such a magnificent view.

We searched out other small ruins. There were no trails. We scrambled through oak brush, under and around juniper trees, slid off smooth rocks, and finally approached three unnamed ruins all in alcoves. All made by Ancestral Puebloans. All different. Some with stacked stone. Some with dressed stones with careful chinking and mortar. One two-room ruin even had vertical grooves carved into the cliff face to steady an ancient ladder, but the most interesting ruin must have been a shaman's home. It contained an altar and a smooth, rounded fire pit, but there was no ceiling soot.

Fascinated, we spoke in soft tones, studying the ancient workmanship, lost in our own thoughts, aware of our mortality, yet keenly, vividly alive as we turned and twisted and climbed to explore. The sky darkened. Rain was coming and we had to get out of the cliff dwellings and quickly down to our horses. We scrambled and slid on decades of dry ponderosa pine needles, laughing now, exhilarated, hungry for dinner and the comfort of camp chairs.

Then we saw the curtain of rain coming up Mancos Canyon. Luckily, it held off until we were almost in our saddles. Sweet wet sage permeated the air. Tired, bruised, dusty, and now wet, we had wanted an adventure and had had one. Everyone slept well that night, but the rain did not stop. On the last day we rode out of the canyon and our supply wagon tipped over. Working as a team we righted the wagon, got back on our horses, lowered our hat brims and trotted towards the rising Mancos River. Outfitter Anne Rapp knew we were wet as drowned ducks. Out of her saddle bag she produced two pine knots rich with resin. Under old pinon trees wranglers found dry wood and soon we had a warm fire to ward off hypothermia. We passed around a bottle of rum and finished off a spice cake. Back in the saddle, we rode two abreast dreading what we'd find where Weber Canyon met the Mancos River.

Ever the consummate guide, Rapp slowly walked her horse across first. From her saddle, she studied the currents, wave trains, and a dangerous sandbar. She rode back, rushing water breaking against her stirrups. Without saying a word, just by her actions, her coolness and her confidence, we knew we could do it. The wagon went next. We held our breath. As it moved into the fast-flowing water it stayed steady and as Willie Richardson, the wagon master, slapped the reins and the two big Belgians pulled the wagon up the muddy bank on the other side, we let out a cowboy yell. Then one at a time, we crossed. That was a record rainfall. In canyon country averaging seven inches of precipitation a year, we had 1.73 inches of rain in 24 hours. That's why the creeks flooded and the wagon slid and tipped. We were lucky to get out.

In the 1940s, Chief Jack House risked the ire of his people by not letting them permanently settle in Mancos Canyon and by not permitting any changes to the canyon floor or canyon rim. Today Ute guides lead all day tours into an unspoiled canyon. Visitors sense the rhythms of Ancestral Puebloan life and walk single file beside remote clusters of stone rooms tucked deep into canyon alcoves to utilize southern exposure in winter and maximize water runoff during spring and summer rains.

Home to a shaman who guided his people, Eagle's Nest ruin towers above Mancos Canyon with full southern exposure and a square of white ochre painted on the shaman's house indicating his power and prestige to travelers. Grappling with an overwhelming sense of vertigo, visitors ascend a steep ladder to walk along the sandstone ledge of Eagle's Nest where a granary still stands with its original small stone door hand-tapered for a perfect fit. Juniper poles jut out from walls. From the top of Eagle's Nest, Mancos Canyon opens to the east and west. A millennia ago anyone on foot could easily have been detected. Standing on the narrow ledge at Eagle's Nest, gazing into those dusty rooms, our modern preoccupation with time has no apparent purpose. In Mancos Canyon centuries have passed and will pass again with little disturbance of the landscape. The view the Ancestral Puebloans beheld remains complete and unaltered. All is silence and sunlight.

Years after our horseback expedition I returned to the park. We drove a van instead of riding horseback, and we hiked to remote sites. One of the best guides is Rickey Hayes, who knows his sites and coaxes stories from stones. A guide with patience, a sense of humor, and a deep knowledge of Puebloan sites learned from Hopi elders, Hayes tells me, "I like coming out here. I like the quietness and spirituality."

"The world changes around us but not in the tribal park," explains Hayes who has guided for thirty seasons. "I enjoy telling people how the Anasazi used to live. They respected each other's circle." As we stand near a rock art site that Hayes gets ready to interpret, he states, "Here in the park the world comes to us. People from different countries come to our area. I tell them how Indians see the world and what was passed down from our grandfathers. We still do our traditions. My son and I still do the sundance." Then he jokes, "In the old days we had a lot of trading posts, but now we go to Wal-Mart."

That's the strength of Hayes' presentations. He skillfully weaves the past and the present to provide a Native worldview on thousand-year-old sites. Visitors listen and ask questions. He answers every one. "If someone asks me a good question," he says, "it pops up all sorts of old stories." One fall morning we waited under a rock shelter as rain turned to tiny ice and graupel. He began to sing and soon the sun burst through clouds and mist. We've been to Inaccessible House in Navajo Canyon, Bone Awl Site in Soda Canyon, Hoot Owl House in Pine Canyon with its Moki steps, and Casa Colorado. "Some of these remote sites I only see 2-3 times a year. Who knows how many little sites are up there?" he tells me.

We drove high up out of the Mancos River Valley and along the canyon rim to Porcupine House with its 60 rooms and four kivas. To the ancients, Hayes made a respectful gift of water, and we quietly entered the site. Rickey and his son showed us a rare Ancestral Puebloan sandal hidden beneath a rock and not in museum storage. The rest of our small group walked further down the cliff ledge, but I stayed behind breathing in the coming fall, smelling the cooler air, watching willow and oak brush leaves scatter in the slight breeze perhaps moved by spirits of the Ancestral Puebloans.

I stood in silence thinking about living 800-years-ago in this tight canyon, sheltered by ponderosa pines, drinking from water seeps, planting corn on the canyon rim above. At these hidden village sites across the Colorado Plateau time seems to stop. Nature prevails. Children's laughter from centuries ago is now the descending bird song notes of a canyon wren and the soft soughing of wind in the tops of pines.

Andrew Gulliford is a professor of History at Fort Lewis College in Durango, Colorado. He is an award-winning author and editor who has won the Colorado Book Award, the New Mexico-Arizona Book Award, the Wrangler Western Heritage Award for Outstanding Non-Fiction from the National Cowboy Museum in Oklahoma City, and the Best Book of the Year Award from the Utah Historical Society.

Baptism in the Anthropocene

Geneva Toland

this is the way to the small-pooled pond.
    this is the way to the wilting.

I've watched a forest burn. I've watched elk and deer mouse scurry.
I've held a wet rag to my nose, and walked towards the flame
without any way to put it out. I see you, apology. Come closer.

this is the way to the fresh-scarred trunk.
this is the way to the glinting.

In the spring, the rains slid the burnt hill down the valley.
The creek grew thick with ash. I bathed myself in the black and emerged
loosed in skin. As the world heats, I heat. As the world burns, I burn.

this is the way to the mud-filled mouth.
this is the way to the melting.

They say heat gives you nightmares. Gives you reason to wreck.
Chokes your airways. Clogs the path. If so, then here—I offer this nightmare.
My broken bleating, my lost. Here—I surrender to suffocation.

this is the way to the dawn-thrush song.
this is the way to the whale-grief belting.

If I am to love this world (and I must) then let it be a wet & slick
sort of love. A sweat. A burn. Let your elbows graze mine
and mix our waters. o little one. o safety. o streambed. o heat.

this is the way to the world, my love.
this is the way to the faulting.

Geneva Toland is a writer, farmer, naturalist, and educator currently working towards her MFA in Poetry at the Institute for American Indian Arts. Her writing has appeared in Southern Humanities Review, Camas, humana obscura, Canary Literary Magazine, and West Trade Review, among others. She feels humbled to live in the juniper and piñon pine foothills of the La Platas, homelands of the Ute, Diné and Puebloan peoples. See her other offerings at www.genevatoland.com. Baptism in the Anthropocene was originally published in Camas Magazine.

This Glitch in Time

Anne Benson

We're headed to the vortex today. I'm having a hard time getting my head around this, but it's one of Dad's last requests, so here we are. In Sedona, Arizona, aka Hippietown. My brothers are acting like this is the most natural thing in the world; Sam's been joking around the whole time.

"Hey, Scout. Get to shoot anybody yet?"

I just nod at him while he grins at me over his shoulder. I'm 18 months into a four-year stint with the Air Force. I've been at Hill Air Base since Basic, and Sam thinks it's great fun to tease his big sister. He knows I'm a decent shot, but he also knows that I've never shot at a live target. I couldn't even shoot the rattler that was sunning itself on a boulder by the creek a few years ago.

I was just settling in at Hill when Greg called with Dad's diagnosis. Easter was the last time I'd made it home, and Dad was fading fast at that point. He died in early June. Pancreatic cancer. He was only 51.

Greg, the oldest, has been taking care of everything. Now he's just driving. Quiet as usual, messing with the radio. No USGS maps on this trip. The Subaru's GPS will get us there.

The flight from Salt Lake was quick, at least. Only a few bumps as the San Francisco Peaks drifted by. But now my stomach's doing flip flops on these switchbacks between Flagstaff and Sedona. I'll claim shotgun on the way home to Cortez.

The trailhead parking lot is full, with groups of people packing it in or heading up the trail. Cars are parked along the road, so Greg pulls around and waits for a Jeep that's leaving. Who knew this place would be so popular?

With all these people, I'm starting to wonder about the legality of our task today. Are you allowed to spread human remains on public land? Plus a Google search told me that this particular site is sacred to the Yavapai-Apache. So there's that.

Sam is atypically subdued as he grabs his pack and hands me a water bottle.

"The trail's pretty short," he says. "Maybe a mile and a half."

October is a good time of year to be in these red rocks. The sun is less intense, and the car thermometer reads a mild 75 degrees. Sparse juniper and piñon dot the scene, scenting the dusty, dry air. A red-tailed hawk screeches in the distance. Six-inch lizards scuttle across the path toward shady rock crevices. One perches atop a rock and warns us to keep our distance by bobbing in a quick staccato.

I can't really call this a hike. More like the proverbial walk in the park. Greg and Sam have small day packs and I'm carrying a bottle of water that I'm not sure I'm going to need. The trail rises slightly from the parking lot, probably less than 200 feet to the top. I think we look normal, just three siblings on an outing to the Boynton Canyon Vortex. We're not wearing yoga pants or playing Native flute, but still we fit in. Sort of. And let's face it, none of these people are going to call the authorities.

"What are we going to do when we get there?" Sam asks. "Just dump him?" Greg glances back at his little brother and shakes his head. Sam, apparently not in the mood to continue his jest, slumps back into his stride.

About a mile up the trail, Greg turns to say, "The Vortex is supposed to be between two rock formations at the end of the trail. You can see Kachina Woman from here." He nods his head toward the narrow stand of rocks at the top of the trail. "It'll be too busy up there."

Greg looks back down the trail and steps off into a shallow juniper-lined wash. Disappearing around a large boulder, he calls back, "This'll do!"

Sam and I glance at each other. He shrugs and follows Greg into the gully. I can see a few people sunning on rocks or leaning on hiking poles near Kachina Woman. Two women pose in downward dog. No one's coming up the trail behind us.

A shadow darkens my shoulder, and I look up to see the hawk stalled almost directly above me. Her golden eye meets mine and we consider each other briefly before she arcs away in widening circles toward the distant cliffs. A final screech rouses eerie notes from the flautist whose mournful tones echo through the canyon. Fitting.

Greg stands near an old juniper, half-dead and twisted. He has a camping shovel in hand, and the forest green box with Dad's ashes rests on the ground. He nods toward a small, prickly hollow at the base of the tree.

"What's the plan?" I ask.

Greg sets down the shovel, takes the plastic bag out of the box, and fiddles with the twist tie. "I don't know. Let's just scatter some around this tree and bury the rest."

Sam and I watch as he digs a small pit and tips the bag into the hole. About half of Dad empties out. The rest Greg shakes around the tree and out into the gully. He shovels a few scoops of dirt onto the pile in the hole and crumples the plastic bag. The three of us stare down at Dad's grave.

"There you go, Dad," Sam whispers.

"Rest in peace," Greg adds.

I should be crying. I'm looking down at the small mound of dusty red dirt where my dad is buried, and my eyes are dry. My heart and stomach are clenching in on each other, but no tears come. Have the boys cried? What would it be like to be wailing in grief?

Heading back to the car, Sam puts a long arm around my shoulders. "This sucks," I say, and tuck into his chest.

We're back on the road when I think to ask the question that's been bugging me since Greg told me about Dad's last wish. "Why here? I mean, why Sedona? And at a vortex?" They pretend not to hear.

"Maybe we should get a room for the night," Sam suggests.

"It's still pretty early," Greg says. "We can stop in Tuba City if we need to, but I'd rather just get home. And don't forget Waylon."

"Tell me!" I demand.

Greg catches Sam's eye in the rearview and barely shakes his head.

"I saw that. Tell me!"

"Mom's not dead," Sam says softly as he turns to look out the window.

"What?"

"At least that's what Dad thought," he adds.

I glare at Greg. "What, she's living in Sedona with some guru or something? And he never told us?"

"It's not like that," Greg says, glancing at me.

"So, what is it?"

"Dad thinks she went back in time," Sam blurts.

"Back in time? You're kidding, right?"

Sam just shrugs. The tires rumble on the recently chip-sealed highway that runs through the Navajo reservation. A southbound pick-up throws a stone, hitting the windshield and breaking through the ambient noise with a crack.

"Damn it. I just got a new windshield." Greg turns to me. "Dad left instructions about some letters that we're supposed to read together. We don't know anything else."

Mom's not dead? She went back in time? What are they talking about? My only memories of her are so faded, I'm not sure she ever even existed in my world. I remember small bits. A voice encouraging me to bite into a carrot just pulled from the soil. Laughter, and the clink of silverware coming from the kitchen. The sound of the bathroom faucet running, and her shh-shh noises helping me find the right muscles to pee. I was five when she disappeared. Eight when Dad put the marker in our memorial garden under the cottonwoods. I'm sure Sam doesn't remember a single thing about her, and Greg never mentions her name.

We're mostly quiet the rest of the way home. Passing the Towaoc casino, Greg says, "I need to get back to work on Monday. And I'm thinking I should move back to Durango soon. Sam, are you able to stay at the house until we get all this under control?"

"I guess," Sam says. "They cancelled my last San Juan run with the water so low. I think it's less than a hundred CFS. And they won't need me at Purg until Thanksgiving."

"My flight's out of Cortez Sunday morning," I say. "I might be able to get more time, if you think I need to."

"Let's see what the letters say and go from there," Greg suggests.

We pull into the house around midnight, just as a healthy-looking skunk waddles across the driveway. Two amber eyes shine back at us in the headlights before he ducks into the culvert. "Better keep Waylon in the back," Sam says.

Waylon is Dad's 10-year-old yellow lab. He carries a few extra pounds and greets us like he hasn't seen a human in months. Body wagging and tail thumping furniture, walls, and legs, he bullies his way between and under, all the while grinning up at us.

Sam lets him out and waits just outside the back door, staring into the night while Waylon takes care of business.

"I'm beat," I say after Sam calls Waylon back inside. "Going up." I see Sam sink into the recliner and switch on the TV before I head upstairs. Waylon's settling by his side and nosing his hand.

I crawl into bed, but I'm too wired to sleep. I can't stop thinking about what Sam said and wondering how the three of us will deal with this. I must have fallen asleep at some point because when I open my eyes, pink and purple clouds greet me through the open shade. How's that go? Pink sky in morning, sailor take warning?

I come downstairs at 7:30, and the TV is still on. Sam's sound asleep, and I can hear Waylon's toenails clicking in the kitchen. Greg's watching the last drips of coffee fill the pot. We mumble a few words and I pour myself a mug before stepping outside into the cool morning air. Waylon bounds out in front, and I wander toward the grove of cottonwoods that shade our memorial garden.

We grew up here, on the Morelli family homestead. Five acres of mostly bottom land along McElmo Creek, protected by sandstone canyon walls, and just outside of Cortez. Over the years, my family transformed this semi-arid plot into a slice of heaven with a small orchard, grapevines, and gardens all connected by pea gravel and stone-lined pathways. The memorial garden at the west end is dotted with granite stones, marking the lives of three generations of Morellis, including Mom.

Dad's marker is already engraved:

Joseph G. Morelli

February 5, 1960 – June 11, 2010

Loving son, father, and husband

Trisha, my love, I will look for you always

What the hell? I will look for you always?

"Waylon! Come!"

I want to ask about the inscription, but when I get back to the house, Greg and Sam are in the dining room with four army-green metal ammo boxes lined up on the table.

"What's all this?"

"It's from Dad," Greg says. "Here's the packet from the lawyer, and here's Dad's letter."

"Can I see the letter?" I take it and read aloud:

Dear Greg, Marla, and Samuel,

I'm sorry I've been so cryptic, but I've been doing this for so long and it's so strange that I thought you should be together when I explained what happened to your mother. The ammo boxes in the garden shed are filled with letters and photos, but I ask that you not open them until you read these two letters.

"Two letters?"

"Read on," Greg says. "He says where the second one is."

Your mom was always searching for some spiritual guidance. She tried churches and temples and synagogues. She sought out mystics and mediums and gurus. When she disappeared, she was on a "vision quest" in Sedona to the vortex where you were to leave my ashes. She didn't return home when she had planned, so I went to Sedona to get a search going. I thought she might have injured herself on the trail, but feared something more sinister had happened. All they found was her car at the trailhead. No trace of her. I thought either she didn't want to be found or something horrible had happened. I searched for three years and finally gave up. That's when we placed the stone marker in the grove.

But then, in 1994, I found a letter from her in the garden shed. It was dated 1982. The letter was an apology, and an explanation of sorts. She wrote that she had slipped back in time by 12 years and was apparently living on an alternate timeline where she never meets me.

It was all very hard to believe, so I wrote her an angry letter and put it in the shed where I found hers. I found a letter every month after that, and I started writing back, thinking that, if she was truthful, it might be 12 years before she would read my messages. I was eventually convinced and started doing research on time travel, hoping to find a way to return her to us. My death will have put an end to that. In any case, we had both lost hope.

I have two requests of you three. The first you will have already completed, and my ashes will be somewhere in the vicinity of the Boynton Canyon Vortex. The second is that you forgive your mother and try to grasp the strangeness of this reality.

The letters and photos in the ammo boxes will explain, in her words and in mine, her altered life from that October day in 1989, and how I came to believe. The letter on the top of the box with the Tom Petty Wildflowers sticker is a letter to you that she wrote in 1996.

All my love and best hopes, Dad

"Did you guys read Mom's letter already?" I'm pacing and feel like I might hyperventilate.

"Sit down, Marla," Greg says. "We haven't looked in the boxes yet."

The Tom Petty box rattles with the sound of beads or small stones rolling around as I slide it closer and flip the latches. The metal hinges creak as I slowly open the box. The boys sidle closer for a better look.

It's filled to the rim with envelopes and photographs. On top is a yellowed envelope with our names printed neatly across the middle. Just under this envelope is a faded Polaroid of Mom.

"Is that our pet cemetery?" Sam asks, referring to our memorial garden that has also received the remains of various pets over the years.

"Looks like," Greg says as he brings the photo to the window to study it. "She's standing next to a stone marker, but it's not hers. Can't quite make out the name."

Sam and I join him at the window, and Sam takes the photo.

"It says, 'Joseph Samuel,' I think. Then maybe, 'April 1986 to May 1986'? And at the bottom, 'Infant son of Joseph and Tamina Morelli.'"

"Here," Sam says, and he hands the photo to Greg, who glances at it before returning Sam's stunned gaze.

"That's the year I was born," Sam whispers. "And Tamina? That's not Mom."

Someone had printed a date in the white space below the photo. It reads 'Oct 1986.'

Waylon barks outside the back door, jolting us out of our stupor. "I got him," I say. Waylon bounds in and wriggles up to Sam at the table and Sam automatically scratches the big dog's head. Both he and Greg simply stare at the ammo boxes as I come to the table. "Mom's letter?" I ask. Greg points, and I unfold the single, hand-written sheet and start reading.

March 1996

Dearest Greg, Marla, and Samuel,

As I write this, you are still young children, so I've asked your father to hold it back until you are better equipped to understand. Not that I understand any of it.

Please know that I didn't mean to leave you. I would not have abandoned my beautiful family, my beautiful children. I fell asleep during a meditation at the vortex in 1989 and woke in an unfamiliar 1977. Your father and I have been trying all these years to find the route back to you. I know now that I'll never return to my own time, to your time, and my heart aches every day because of it.

When I made it back to Cortez, I began writing letters to your father every month. I put them in a tin in the garden shed hoping that during his Fall chores, he'd find them. I was so thrilled when I received that first letter. But any hope I once had left me long ago.

He said he'd eventually give you all our letters so that you'd know what happened. I hardly know myself.

I will keep writing. I hope that you will write your own someday so that

I can know you and know how each of you has grown.

I hope you can feel all the love I have for you across this glitch in time that separates us.

Love, Mom

"This can't be real," I say. I feel like I may start that sobbing, wailing thing.

Sam opens a second ammo box and fans through a stack of photos of us as kids. "This must be a box of Dad's letters," he says.

"I think it's real." Greg shakes his head and looks over at me. "I don't know how, but I think it's real."

A sob rattles my chest and my cheeks are wet. Waylon nudges my elbow and I half-smile down at him.

"Hand me that box."

Anne B. Benson has stamped soles onto shoes in a dusty New England factory, cleaned rooms at a Holiday Inn, waited tables from New Hampshire to Florida to Arizona, sold real estate in a tiny northern lake town, edited a weekly newspaper, taught at an elementary school, and worked for an environmental nonprofit. She writes in the Four Corners region of Colorado where she lives with her husband and the best doggone dog in the West.

The empty space of him*

Elizabeth Long

He lived a big life –
international science,
weapons in space,
his family in the wings.

He brought us back elaborate jokes,
sour after repetition.
A whiff of a wider world:
bagels, strong cheese, strange aperitifs,
a taste for eccentric foreign cars.

I lived in the beam
of occasional attention:
he taught me mumblety-peg
behavior of zero
love of Jane Austen

ambition
inadequacy.

But he was better on the big screen.

He put my mother in a small box
and sucked the air out 1950s style.
Squashed my brother,
with dismissive abruptness –
made me his sunflower daughter,
and happy to be so.

They put his ashes in the ground.
But the empty space of him still lives and grows
as I, like a backwards spider,
unspin the thorny web of who he was.
And why I loved him so.

* From a poem by Neeta Nadkarny

Elizabeth Long has Western roots in her grandparents' generation, but grew up in Ithaca, NY, worked in Manhattan after college, got involved in the social movements of the 70's, and then became a professor of sociology at Rice University. She adopted a baby and became a proud mother, then met and married her husband of 28 years, Bill, and became a proud and fun stepmother and grandmother to a medium-sized but not average family. Elizabeth and Bill retired to Durango, and she is engaged in the community and the great outdoors, and started writing poetry again.

Lions, Dogs, and Inner Monologues

Maddy Butcher

I was helping gather calves on New Year's Day. I had my two dogs with me and was riding my grey horse, Ray. The country was rough, full of piñon, juniper, and scrub oak, and the area was good-sized, about a square mile, so my friend and I had split up and I was sussing out a small, narrow canyon alone. By sussing out, I mean that I suspected the calves were down in the canyon, grazing their way east, and I was zigging and zagging, trying to find a way down its craggy walls.

The sides were steep, mostly unpassable, and I was riding cautiously, having to back up and turn around often. My dog, Tina, jogged across a room-sized boulder jutting out over the gully and I snapped a picture to remember the frustrating going. We paused and listened for animals moving. Then I watched, big-eyed, as an adult mountain lion strode up the other side of the canyon, some hundred feet away. She walked purposively but without urgency. Large, lanky, and with that long tail, she moved with grace, efficiency, and power. I soaked in the sighting with as much focus as I could muster. Not taking my eyes off her, not moving or reaching for my phone. A minute later, I saw another one (another one!), a juvenile, following the adult at a distance.

I've lived in cat country for more than a decade and I know well the feeling - in your bones and in your mind - that you are being seen by them (also by deer, bear, hawks, ravens, and hares, of course) but I'd not laid eyes on one until now. It was a bodily experience - like running a race or speaking publicly on a stage – buzzing mind, fizzing senses. And because I'm a writer, the old brain was in overdrive, witness to the witnessing, trying to commit to memory what I saw and heard and felt.

It wasn't until later, heading home in the truck, that I realized it was five years to the day since I'd found my beloved dog, Belle, killed by a lion.

Belle was a 12-year-old Bassett Hound mutt, with short legs and a long history of civil disobedience. Her sense of smell was powerful. Her sense of hearing less so. The almighty nose demanded more attention than my calls ever did. I loved her dearly, through gritted teeth.

Her AWOL excursions were many and storied, but thankfully, old age was slowing and shortening them. She didn't take off as much as she just dawdled.

On New Year's Eve, as day turned to dusk, she went walking with us down the quiet road near the house. When I last saw her alive, she was bounding like a puppy, big ears flapping; she'd caught a scent and was following it with obvious glee. I figured she'd come home in due course, stand at the door, and give me that high-toned woof to be let in.

She never did.

In the dirt and snow, we searched that night, the next morning, and the next afternoon for a forty-pound dirt-and-snow-colored dog.

Turns out Belle had a parting lesson for me: *Respect a Dog's Nose.* I finally found her, thanks to my younger dogs' sniffers. As I was surveying the country, riding yet another ridge, they stopped to circle and inspect her body. Belle looked asleep and almost unharmed save some blood on her side and her head.

From all indications, this was a mountain lion kill. It had been quick and likely motivated by aggravation, not hunger. Belle pursued it and the cat had disposed of her. I don't harbor any ill will towards the cat. It was doing what cats do. Belle was being Belle.

(I train my dogs not to chase wildlife. Belle was a horrible student.)

It took a while to dig through the frozen ground and shovel deep enough to discourage coyotes from rooting out her body. We buried her on a knoll above the house, under a tree. It was a spot she often chose to survey the neighborhood. I think the old explorer might have approved.

Over these five years, other beloved animals have died. Two years ago, I sat vigil and watched my mom die. She trained dogs, coached skiing, raised her children, learned to sail, and mastered photography. Mom sent me Valentine's Day cards. She liked the poet Mary Oliver who wrote *what do I do with my one wild and precious life?*

Belle and Mom knew what to do. It's taken grief, time, and hindsight for me to get some kind of handle on it. And by "it" I mean living life, preferably with purpose.

I'm a writer. I've spent years and years tapping away at the laptop. I've spent years and years in my head, searching for the best turns of phrase, the best imagery, the best interpretations of research and interviews. Write, rewrite, rewrite, write some more. Polish it. Scrap it. Send to colleagues. Review edits. Begin again.

Lately, though, I'm writing less and riding more. After many unpaid days, in and out of the saddle, fixing fence, getting rained on, losing hats and phones, I now get paid to ride, work fence, fight with scrub oak, and ask my dogs to fetch that lagging cow. I barely get minimum wage, I go through gloves and jeans quickly, and I'm excited by the things I can do.

To people who aren't familiar with cowboying, it's hard to explain the work. Mostly, it's about paying attention and being resourceful because I'm often by myself, far from anything, with only wits, an able body, my animals, and perhaps a pair of pliers.

Friends and family question my occupational pivot and that, too, can be hard to explain. Writing for a national paper is a good gig. It's required skills honed over three decades: how to cultivate sources, how to interview, how to whittle a big topic down to 800 words and how to make those 800 words interesting. It's an inside gig, which is nice when it's cold or wet or windy. Or cold *and* wet *and* windy.

But I wonder if any of us is making a difference. I see great writers and great work ignored and pithy writers and click bait worshipped. What I think is interesting is not what other people think is interesting. It's big picture angst, but it's also personal: I get despondent about whether I contribute to society or offer an original voice.

Do I? Am I?

These cases are argued over and over, in a courtroom of one, in my head. I poll my peeps about the merits of the work we do, how to balance making money with feeling good about it. First-world problems and lucky to have them. Anyway, the jury, my jury, is still out. *Heck if I know, I'll just keep moving.*

Swapping writing for riding has been good yet unsettling to mind, body, and spirit. I ride well, but it's humbling to know eight-year-olds who rope better than me. I can't stick a buck. I get cold and hungry and desperately need to pee way sooner than my boss. Sometimes, I have to text myself details lest I forget the order of things to get done.

It hasn't escaped me that I was safer, in many ways, inside, on a computer. But maybe being less safe is what I needed and what I need. Maybe the writing, the grief over aforementioned deaths, the hours in the saddle, and the hindsight have all brought me here, to a place I appreciate.

This land, these animals, this work - they all require me to be here now, not in my head, not heading down virtual rabbit holes but actually, really, looking out for rabbit holes and prairie dog holes.

Some things I've learned:

I know shit. As in scat. This is handy when thinking about what's out there with you on any particular day or week.

I know how quickly it gets cold up on the west fork of the Dolores after the sun goes down. Nearly a degree a minute.

I know how long it takes to move cows off that one park on Stoner Mesa and to the orange gate and I know that a few will always peel off to the south and it's best to head them off before they even ponder the notion.

I can speak to my dogs with my eyes.

I can bring a horse from uncatchable and unrideable to somewhat reliable. His name is Table and he's awesome.

I know that bulls can be randy and ornery, but when they're done for the season, they're done. This can make them hard to find over, say, the entire side of a mountain.

This isn't the end of the story. I will continue to learn. I will get better. I will get hurt and I will fuck up. I will see mountain lions. I may write about them. But will it matter if I don't?

Maddy Butcher is a free-lance journalist with occasional op-ed pieces in the Washington Post. She also day works for Montezuma County ranchers.

Winter in Dolores as a Child

Ellen Hill Robinson

When it fell, thick, wet,
I was in its middle:
mouth open, hands limp in mitten socks at my sides,
heedless,
head held dizzy back to count each flake,
but they, winning,
licked my face.

When it stayed, I walked on it
carefully, oh so precariously, stepping as lightly as I could
on top of the thin crust of ice, so assured
my weight would never break it, and no one would ever die.

When it melted, I watched for icicles,
broke them, and licked them like Popsicles,
my tongue sticking hot at first,

then, swimming fast, cool to the tip;
there, dizzy still,
I caught each
drop.

And when it came again
I dragged out my thrift-store hockey skates,
made clumsy-eights and moons on the river's awkward ice;
and then with sugar, vanilla, an egg,
and the purest of snow,
my sister and I made sweet cream.

Never ever
did ugly, old cold interrupt
or threaten
such delicious play.

Ellen Hill Robinson is a teacher and writer, born and raised in the Four Corners now dividing her time between the Denver area and Dolores. Her family homesteaded near Cortez in 1909 and her kin have lived and breathed the Four Corner's enchantment ever since.

Apogee

Sam Tezak

Ixto first sensed the vessel's high, sheltering presence as it crossed Heaven's River. Single-celled and gelatinous, Ixto expanded in Garra's observation tower to feel the outside craft trudge through space. Its hulking shape cast a penumbra over the amoeba's ship, and entered its consciousness like dread.

For millennia, Ixto and its exoskeleton, Garra, scuttled across the silent floor of the galaxy's furthest reaches. It absorbed the infinite murmurs of stars' birth and decay and planets reduced to gaseous elements. Until now, when a foreign spacecraft emerged and staked out the amoeba's first memory against the long, dark night.

Dozens of drones shuttle out from Garra, each one manned by Ixto, and they encircle the mysterious spacecraft. Inside Garra, the exoskeleton hums with information collected by the drones. The vessel measures 2,180 meters in length, 1,460 meters in width, and is estimated to weigh 8,916 metric tons. Scopes from the drones probe the mass encased by metal crenulations which appear to undulate across the craft. Centimeter-by-centimeter the probes scrape the crenulations, seeking any suggestion of an opening or electronic activity.

The ship seems interminable as it stretches into blackness. Eventually, one of the scopes begins to transmit a low din which amplifies through Garra. The scope pursues the noise for several meters until it locates the source of the sound. A large handle emerges between the scales. Ixto instructs the drone to prize the latch open.

On entering, Ixto feels the sense of listening to a fugitive space. Past the interstices of fuel compartments and engineer rooms, the amoeba enters a vast atrium with lights emanating from the ceiling. A long silence grows and hardens. A strange, four-limbed creature slumps against a wall, unresponsive. The creature's face appears ashen, its digits clasped near its torso. Two orbs, green pricked with black dots, are situated on the face, beneath which the skin slopes outwards. Under which is an opened maw and a flash of square teeth. Horrifying. The creature appears gorgonized.

Ixto sifts through the atrium and expands into the gallery where it climbs along walls filled with images of other creatures, similar in composition to the first one: googly orbs, flaps of skin hanging off the sides of their faces, maws flashing incisors. Images of the frozen creature, smells, and the feeling of the ship transmit back to Garra. As the amoeba excavates other rooms it discovers more creatures preserved in amniotic fluid, locked behind windows which reveal their same timorous, frozen stares. Ixto senses these creatures are abstracted from the world.

A faint noise murmurs in a distant compartment and the mold moves along the hallways to locate the source. At the eve of a cracked door to an indistinct room, a noise trumpets from a speaker. A sound so foreign and rich it seems to spring up in abundance. Ixto moves into the space filled with the sound which gives the distinct impression of wading into some other substance. The sound enraptures Ixto with manifolds of instrumentation and it seems to swim weightlessly within it. As quickly as the sound emerged, it disappears into what can only be described as voices transmitted through space.

. . . afterwards I ended up at the cantina outside of town. Ya know the one, Cookie's.

Sure, I know Cookie's.

I sat at one of the booths and looked out towards Gooseberry.

Rain pocks and dribbles down the windows. At first slowly, and then in sheets. All the houses and the main drag full of glistening neon and ambered in the fall. Rain breaks apart on the roof.

It felt like there was so much God.

It is dark and Stella sits in the darkness with her elbow on her knee, her face resting against the phone.

Billy, what did you do when you arrived at Cookie's?

A waiter walks over to a figure sitting at a rounded table. They tear a receipt from their book and hand it over. The figure sitting at the table flips the check over. Exasperated, they pat their jacket pockets and look up at the waiter.

I downed a couple of margaritas and when the check arrived, I thought I lost my wallet.

Jesus. Did you meet anybody or were you planning to meet anybody when you got there?

Billy rubs her temples and closes her eyes. Stella's line of questioning always puts her on her heels, the way she uses questions to distill answers into blocks of information.

Rain rolls and thunder erupts over the drinking hole. Willie Nelson plays on the jukebox.

The Last Cowboy Song. Do you remember that one?

When Stella responds it sounds as if she held her breath until she couldn't hold it any longer.

No.

Behind her eyelids, Billy sees the reflection of her Citroen's headlights as they cross the cantina's mottled windows. She hears the cascading sound of thunder and the mud sucking beneath her boots. She tries to imagine another life elsewhere – and wonders if it is something in her blood.

Billy, are you still there?

Regulars watch the water fall from the sky and the little room shakes in the storm. Rain forms écriture on the windowpanes. A silhouette pushes away from the table and disappears before re-appearing a few moments later outside. The screen door swings behind them. She watches them light their cigarette: a jacket collar pulled up and their hat pulled down to block the elements. Smoke blooms out and scatters. The storm eases. Chords slip out, another silhouette. The screen door swings closed behind them.

Her voice emerges again over the sound of Billy's memory.

Did you talk to anyone when you arrived?

A dark figure, ember floating and swelling, channels of rainwater in the parking lot.

Billy reaches into her flannel pocket and shakes out a cigarette from a crumpled, half-empty pack.

I really don't want to do this over the phone.

Her fluorescent kitchen light flickers. She pulls her knees closer to her chest and listens to Stella's breath on the other end of the line.

I also don't want to see you again, Billy.

She takes the cigarette to her lips, lights and inhales. She didn't believe any of it, how could she? Outside the house's yellow lights turn off.

Stella, do you remember that winter it snowed?

All you need to do is tell me. All you need to do is tell me.

Let me show you.

Billy zips her jacket as she steps out the theater's double doors and into the parking lot. A thin layer of snow congregated on the cars during the rehearsal. She drives up the fleece-covered lane north, her manuscript tucked inside her jacket pocket and close to her chest. Flakes accumulate like paragraphs on her windshield. Wipers knock them off a few moments later. There are few traffic lights and so she cruises along. Briefly the man on the radio recites commodity prices before disappearing behind poor reception. Thump. More snow calves off the car roof. Multi-colored lights line adobe and wrought-iron fences and circle around cacti and sagebrush.

When she arrives at the cantina, tangled piñon branches obscure the full moon's light. She sits in the darkened car and watches the people mill about. A waiter jots down orders, a couple of kids chase one another through a maze of booths. A young girl leans over a table and sucks cola through a straw. And Stella, who sits by the window, eats an enchilada over a bed of beans and rice. She looks down at her phone – 6:46 – before quickly pocketing it to avoid illuminating the interior of her car.

Cookie's sits along the edge of the Rio Grande, a couple of miles outside of town. A cantina which proudly touts that in its heyday, a celebrity chef crowned it for its green chile burger. Of course this was back before the Departure.

Billy looks at Stella. Recently she's obsessed over telepathy and wonders if it's some extension of empathy. Billy imagines transmitting a message to her through the windshield and into the diner, past all the snow and glass. She doesn't know what she'd say if she could. For a moment she worries she unknowingly can transmit thoughts to others and Stella is listening in. 6:56. Stella finishes her meal. The waiter arrives with the check and Stella produces a bill and he walks away. She leaves the table and walks towards the bathroom. Billy opens the car door and walks inside. 7:00.

I had a dream about you.

Stella looks across from them at the booth. Together, they watch the world go by outside. On countless nights like this one, the pair plays a game of guessing each car as it passes along the road and imagining the lives tucked inside the vehicle. Most cars are American-made trucks and at least 10 years old. And most people are their neighbors, who go together nearly everywhere, circling the local market, the library, and the cantina *ad infinitum*. From their observation window they imagine vintage cars sharing the same roads as flying vehicles. Each one of them shiny and brightly colored, driven by politicians, gangsters, and celebrities.

As if pulling the thread of conversation back into the present, Stella begins again.

I had a dream about you. We were drinking wine at the bottom of the canyon. There was a bird, you called it a black-crowned night heron.

Clarence walks over to their table with a tray of tortilla chips and salsa. Soft-spoken with a gray mustache, the waiter bears an uncanny resemblance to One-Eyed Jim. Save for the fact that Clarence's two eyes are intact. For as far back as Stella can recall, the two men of ambiguous relation to one another occupy the bench outside of the local market from sunrise to sunset. Which is where Billy first met them on one blazing summer day when she arrived in town. She likened them to a pair of gentle gargoyles, gossiping and greeting customers outside of the market.

The special tonight is chicken mole enchiladas with crispy chile relleno. Can I get ya'll anything to drink?

Stella and Billy order a couple of dark lagers and a plate of sopapillas.

We were watching this bird, this heron, fish alongside the bank of the river.

Billy imagines the river. How they sat there all summer watching birds and talking.

We were sitting upstream in our camping chairs and we were drunk. The chair legs kept sinking slowly into the sand until one of us would fall. We kept falling over and over and we were laughing so hard. But the bird stayed perched in the water.

There are yellowed trees and enamel mugs. Billy and Stella make bets on when the bird would snatch a fish from the water. Each time the bird reached out its neck it seemed to stretch longer than the last time until it would retract back into its body.

Suddenly it stretched its neck across the entire river! It must have been thirty or forty feet long and I remember I looked over and you had these wide eyes.

Feathers on the bird's neck waft in the breeze. As it nears the other side it leans its head towards the ground.

It seemed like it was trying to listen to something.

Suddenly it pulls its head back across the water, startled by some noise. It lifts off down the shadow of the river, following its curves.

Then what happened?

I don't recall. But I remember we woke back up in our chairs. Not actually woke up, but in the dream. I looked over and . . .

The sun is gone and it is just the black faces of the cliffs thrown across the water. A figure stumbles along the shore.

I could hear you naming the birds. I thought you were just drunk and full of shit. But you kept calling them out with this sing-song voice, naming each bird. I tried calling to you but kept walking until you were just a shadow and disappeared behind the brush. At first I thought it was funny but then I wasn't sure if you were coming back. I called out louder.

Billy! Billy? Billy! One of the figures stands up from their chair and shouts at the other, walking down the river.

I could hear my own nerves in my voice. Just when I was about to get up and look for you, you burst out of the cottonwood trees next to me. It was getting dark but I could see your wide eyes and the edges of something dangling in your hand.

The figure laughs: I got it! I got it!

You showed me what you were holding. You put it right in front of my face and I could see it was the heron. Dead. Its head smashed in, all limp in your hand.

Stella looks at Billy holding the bird in her hands, horrified. And looks back at Billy. Billy cuts up the bird on a nearby stone. Night grows in the canyon. The pair build a fire with dry grasses, twigs, and branches from the canyon floor. Billy pierces the bird meat with a sharpened stick and sets it near the fire. Stella looks up and sees Billy's working the bird over the flames. She can't see her eyes and the flames flickering between them cast shadows over her face. It was quiet, except for the crackle of the fire.

Then you looked at me and very solemnly told me: We must eat what we fear.

Rain threads the entrance of our cave. Cookie's neon sign fizzles behind the shimmering sheets. Since the beginning, Cookie's belonged to the distance: a cantina dug out at the edge of the world. Somehow its vinyl booths and chimichangas staved off war and famine, civil unrest and even the Departure. How would it handle this?

From the far reaches of our cave, BlueCorn crackles.

Do you see it? Did it come back?

A silhouette ambles past the empty booths and arrives at the stools arranged along the window. It pauses and I squint my eyes. No features, no face – a shadow propped up inside a glass menagerie. I don't trust my sight. The rain muddles everything.

Nah, it's just old Clarence haunting the window.

Does BlueCorn sense it? How my uncertainty lingers and mixes with the perfume of rain and ash. They sputter something incoherent as the storm escalates and obliterates their words. A tin drops into my lap. I feel the papery label and pull the tab to crack it open. The fishy smell of cat food swallows us. My eyes burn as I bring the mush up to my mouth. The silhouette hanging out at the window has disappeared and Cookie's blazes like a lantern behind the storm. When I stare out long enough and soften my eyes, each bite can taste like fajitas sizzling on cast iron.

BlueCorn and I, we found each other the way lovers do, stumbling around in the dark.

Not this dark – another dark – the Rio Carmel superfire. Scorched earth kind of shit. No survivors. Unless you count us, which feels generous. And now we sit in the maw of oblivion watching Cookie's last customers wander into and out of its glass doors. BlueCorn extends a ghoulish arm into the storm. Raindrops slip across the skin – pocked, melted, and hairless.

As the rain eases, a figure emerges and stands beneath the red sign. The last time I saw Billy, we woke up on a bed of glass with the blue sky wheeling around its jagged corners. There was no sound until the sirens erupted in our ears. Billy looked at me, mangy and wild-eyed, blood pooling around her head. Siren lights reflected in the blown-apart windshield. Footsteps approached us.

Angel, she whispered. Angel . . .

I wandered through wildfires and across deserts sucked dry by heat and wind to find the name of that feeling. The surprising realization that it had all caught up to us, how we found ourselves banished to unfamiliar territory.

Wait here, I think I know them.

BlueCorn gurgles but I don't hear them. I slip out of the cave and walk toward the figure. Blood pounds in my ears and I'm glazed in the rain.

As if the chords are woven into the rain, the Red-Headed Stranger croons between thunderclaps. The end of a hundred-year waltz.

Angel.

Sam Tezak is a fifth-generation Coloradan who lives with his wife in Mancos, Colorado. He studied English Creative Writing: Poetry at Colorado College and interned at Copper Canyon Press and Narrative Magazine. He has written poetry and fiction off-and-on over the past decade, and "Apogee" is his first fiction submission.

The Ravens

Jessica Pace

I was still navigating the residuals
of a dark time for which there were still no words
when I arrived
for the last solstice burning.

The effigies stood
three stories tall, an amalgam of the landscape
enwrapped in a Southwestern winter's incense
of juniper, smoke and starlight,
dormancy and frigid defeat.

When night fell and the crowd gathered
the birds rose in a rush
of spark after spark after spark.

I fell into the stream of midwinter mourners

moving clockwise
around the ashes-to-ashes
and dust-to-dust
of their most private pleadings,
molting the darkness.

They're wintering now
but they can see spring.

Jessica Pace lives in the Four Corners. Her poems have been published in a smattering of random literary journals.

· E S S A Y ·

The Joyous Cries of Children Playing

Kevin T. Jones

Seven years ago my wife Barbara Evert and I moved to remote Montezuma County, Colorado. We fled the exponential growth of Salt Lake City and the frenetic rush of traffic, zooming between stoplights and racing along the freeways, which often slowed to the speed of a sloth. The shimmering fumes of Chevron's best choking our lungs and pores, and dreary winter inversions drove us away, to a place with clean air and few people. Very few people. The Four Corners.

We found a beautiful, hand-built off-grid home on 42 acres nestled in a canyon, surrounded by Piñon-Juniper forest. We are two miles from a paved road, and ringed by farms and ranches. Our 42 acres seems like much more, as the neighboring farmers can't till the rugged rocky canyon slopes that surround and protect us. A perennial stream runs through our property and wildlife abounds—we've seen deer, elk, coyotes, bobcats, mountain lions, black bears, and a grand abundance of birds, from bald eagles and wild turkeys to goldfinches and nuthatches. No streetlights or neighbors to pollute our night skies, we have views of the heavens few places can rival. Our quarter-mile driveway rarely sees a vehicle—invited guests and delivery drivers are our only visitors.

But the most notable difference between our new home and the city we left behind is what we hear. Or don't hear. In the city, even late at night, we could always hear the hum of the freeways, accentuated by the occasional blurt of a semi's diesel, or the scream of a rocket bike through six gears and 120 miles per hour. During the day we had the usual comings and goings of neighbors, garbage trucks, police sirens, and passenger planes coming and going from the international airport. The summer seemed to bring an endless celebration of some sort with explosions of roman candles, dazzling blasts of sparks and colored flames, and the pow pow pow of Black Cats and bottle rockets that terrified our pets did little to enhance our appreciation of the holidays.

When we moved we were delighted to hear, once the noise of people and their machines was lessened, the subtle sounds of a breeze through the Junipers, the descending call of a canyon wren, the yipping of a family of coyotes, the piercing cry of a red-tailed hawk, and the sublime, subdued natural essence of place. The overall effect invites effortless contemplation, enhanced relaxation, and profound appreciation for the incredible natural world, our home.

We live in a place where I can go in any direction from our home and pee without any chance of anyone seeing me and taking offense. Our nearest neighbor is a good friend who lives a quarter mile away, and out of sight. The county road we live on dead-ends just past her home at the entrance to the ranch that has been worked and nurtured by the same family for generations. Beyond the ranch stretches the vast Canyons of the Ancient National Monument wilderness. We got away from the city and its sometimes overwhelming ocean of humanity, its noise, light, and air pollution. We got away from it all.

We were often asked if we would miss the people, and, of course we knew we would miss our friends, and the cherished communities we had become part of and embraced over the years. But no, we knew we wouldn't miss the *people*, the masses of people that surrounded us and swept us along like a powerful current. No, we wouldn't miss them. We do not miss them.

And what we found is that we have not landed in a human vacuum, a deserted expanse of nobody but us. No, that is not the case at all. We have made many friends and we embrace the rural ethic of always looking out for others, of neighbors being neighborly. The ready assistance available in cities—for flat tires, medical issues, plumbing and heating problems, and a convenience store on every corner—is simply not available here.

In addition to enjoying the company of new friends and neighbors, we soon began to see, among the sage and rabbitbrush, the sumac and scrub oaks, the humanity that envelops our home. Starting with a few potsherds scattered on the ground, and then the walls of a tower as tall as a person, the chipped stone and charcoal stains eroding from a gentle slope, we became aware of the rich and omnipresent reminders that we are not alone, we are not the first, and will not be the last to live here, to love this place, to be part of it, to live among the trees, the stones, the gentle breezes and raging winds of the great sage plain. We realized that we are part of a tradition, an ongoing human thread from the distant past to the infinite future. We are not alone.

I have long been aware of the shreds and patches of ancient cultures that remain, that remind us of a past that may not be apparent to the unobservant. I am trained as an anthropologist--one who studies people and their culture. In my specialty, I still study people, although the people I study may have lived long ago and are not around to talk with about their cultures, their lifeways, their behavior. They did, however, leave clues.

On our land we have artifacts reaching back many thousands of years. The base of a lanceolate projectile point, the edges ground to avoid cutting the sinew that lashed it to a foreshaft has lain in place for some 8,000 years. Large hafted bifaces attest to use as cutting and piercing tools by archaic peoples, hunter-gatherers who roamed these canyons over 2,000 years ago.

More recent artifacts and features reflect the presence of Ancestral Puebloan peoples, likely related to the modern Puebloan tribes, and less ancient artifacts are evidence of the historic tribes of the region, most notably the Ute, Navajo, Apache and Paiute. The marks left by the Ancestral Puebloans and modern tribes are most abundant, while those of the earlier citizens have been weathered, scattered, and sometimes lost in the sands of time. The most recent evidence of prior inhabitants include initials scratched in the soft standstone of a small rock shelter above the creek: WD 11, and ELS 11 made their marks there in 1911. There is also a modern midden area--a scatter of trash perhaps as much as a hundred years old, once discarded, but now bearing testament to the lives lived here through rusted tractor parts, bed frames, cracked and shrinking shoe soles, bottles and jars that once contained food, medicine, and beverages, and an occasional child's toy.

In my graduate studies I was privileged to be able to live among hunter-gatherers in South America and study how their behavior left artifacts and features that would be accessible to archaeologists years later. It is a field known as ethnoarchaeology. Because I lived among people I knew and loved, I began to see archaeological sites, even ones thousands of years old, in terms of their representation of human behavior. When I see a stone wall, I also see the hands and labor that went into creating it, carrying and shaping heavy stones, mixing mud mortar, building a home to shelter a family. When I see the stained earth in an ancient hearth, I see people tending that fire, warming themselves, cooking something, shooing away insects. I see people on the landscape, living, thriving, loving, caring for each other, passing along stories, singing, dancing, grieving. And most enriching and gratifying, because among the hunter-gatherers I spent much of my time interacting with and learning from children, when I see traces of the past, I see the young ones, the children, and I hear the joyous cries of them playing. And I smile.

In the Four Corners region we are surrounded by reminders of the past. Reminders of people. The cultures of the area, including ancient ones, are celebrated at places such as Mesa Verde National Park, the Canyons of the Ancients, the Montezuma Heritage Museum, and the Cortez Cultural Center. I invite everyone to ponder the great time depth of humanity represented here, which is still present nearly everywhere you look. Take a moment to see, and to listen. And to hear the joyous cries of children playing. And smile.

Kevin T. Jones is an archaeologist and writer who lives off grid near Pleasant View, Colorado. His recent novel A Quick Trip to Moab *was a finalist for the 2023 Colorado Book Award in general fiction. He served as State Archaeologist of Utah for seventeen years.*

Esa Minúscula y Constante Cadencia

for Reinaldo

Peter Baxter

Trees of the Oriente
trembled at your child touch
when you wrapped them blameless in your blameless arms.
They were the pillars—
you gripped them first.
You climbed them,
their bare skin fibrous against your own
as you sought the secret in the canopy.
Up there in the sway of majesty
the sentinels sighed to you.

They watched you look up at your mother
and your grandmother and your aunts
and once even at your father,
his eyes and his curly dark hair under the wide brim of his hat
as he strode fleeting through the tall grasses

taller then than your life.
They watched you approach others nearer your hut,
carving curving lines into their bark,
giving them names
that shuddered
when your grandfather's axe
pounded relentlessly at them
and sent resignation and farewell
throbbing through their viscous veins.

They watched you go up into the Gibara when you were fourteen
and they watched from afar as you walked into classrooms
and lecture halls and libraries.
They watched you in cafés and cars, on beaches, among waves.
They watched you in prison cells.

They watched you still when you fled
and when you were finally far away and free—
   free to scream in the faces of both systems,
   free to feel snowflakes falling on your own upturned face,
   free to offer and accept the invitation to the dance
  of typewriter keys that tapped out your cadence, tapped out your
    life.

Peter Baxter was born in Durango, Colorado. He lives in Flagstaff, Ar-izona and teaches high school English.

The Winding Road

Shawn McAllister

Not many people drive through these mountains at quarter till four in the morning. Those who do will certainly be familiar with the ominous silence, the peaks rising like suffocating black curtains all around, leaving only a thin sliver of starry sky above. More than anything, it's lonely. There's an unshakeable feeling that you are the only person in the entire world.

Everything about it said, *You shouldn't be here, Sarah.*

The moon was out that night, I think. But it didn't matter. The glare of my headlights shrouded everything else in complete darkness. Every bend I turned revealed nothing. A normal person might wonder how anyone would be crazy enough to speed up this dark highway in the dead of night. I just wondered how it felt to be a normal person.

And so I kept going. I was on edge in the total silence, even more so than when I'd snuck through the house at 2:32 a.m., even more so than when I'd grabbed the keys and crept out into the yard, even more so than when I'd gotten into my parents' new Kia Sorento and backed it out of the driveway. Somehow, the further I got from the scene of my crime, the more anxious I became. But it wasn't the fear of getting caught that made me so tense, it was the eerie emptiness of the vast mountains, not to mention the unsettling silence of the car. It ran way too smoothly for my liking. I guess, given all the money my parents had thrown at it, the seats were pretty comfy. But if fancy cars were all it took to live a happy life, I wouldn't have been here.

The car and I continued to glide up and down the hills, round bend after bend, as if things were okay. Looking at the starlit sky above, I could almost forget everything I was running from. But I knew that if I looked away from the road for too long, I'd find out what the mountains had in store for me. I tried to imagine what they thought of me, a tiny speck of light, passing through their domain for an even tinier speck of time. Those black curtains had been blocking out the moon and stars for thousands of years before I even existed. *People are so small,* I thought.

Soon the right shoulder fell away, leaving an unknowable darkness beside me. I wondered what the speed limit here was. Certainly less than the 64 I was doing. But as I looked at the mountains, they didn't care if I was going 50 or 64 or 75, and so I pushed harder on the gas, knowing in the back of my mind that a sharp turn could kill me.

But a part of me wondered how it would feel to die just like her; a crazy person, alone, in a car at night.

As much as I didn't want to think about her, my thoughts kept straying, imagining scary things. Monsters hiding in the darkness ahead. Her face as she flew through the guardrail and realized she was gonna die . . .

What does it look like to realize you're gonna die? What if you're not ready? She wasn't ready. But she'd been drinking, she always did.

And I loved her, but dammit, she had problems. *Not like I'm much better. But now I'm here and she's not, and who says life is fair?*

Shadows zoomed past, and the only way to know I was going forward was the occasional sign reminding me of how far I was from civilization. My heart jumped a little every time I saw one.

The thought of slowing down tickled the back of my mind, but so did the thought of speeding up. My life didn't seem quite so important out here. I could already see the headlines: "Runaway Girl Killed in Mountain Car Crash," or something. I was no journalist. But two fatal accidents in two days? Oh, they'd have a field day with that.

And there I went, thinking about Becky again. Maybe the faster I drove away from that town, the faster I'd forget. But I couldn't see anything, and I couldn't hear anything, and my imagination had free rein to run wild.

Let me out of here, I thought, leaning back and closing my eyes for a second. But I couldn't keep them closed. Some instinct, buried deep down, made me keep my hands on the wheel.

Then the road turned again. And it didn't stop, it just kept curving, more and more, and I realized I was going too fast. My pulse quickened as I spun the wheel further and further left, and just as the sheer drop-off grew alarmingly close on my right, I heard a low rumbling not far ahead. It began softly, then rose to a thunderous volume.

My heart jumped clear out of my chest as two sharp beams of light came barreling into view. As the vehicle, a semi-truck, roared closer, my ears were overwhelmed by a piercing hiss. Worse still, I could feel the car being pulled toward the towering truck as it raced past.

I jammed on the brakes, but the car was only tugged harder. It seemed like ages before I was free of the truck's pull, and when my eyes regained focus, I found myself almost entirely in the oncoming lane. In a panic, I again spun the wheel, and the road continued turning for another few terrifying moments before finally straightening out.

Gradually, my heart quieted. I took several deep breaths, appreciating that I was still alive, followed by an overwhelming urge to stop. I flung the door open and scrambled out, not even bothering to turn the car off.

The rush of cold air shocked me. Then, once I'd regained my bearings, I ran through the darkness to the side of the road. I stared back at the car, still lit up in the middle of the lane. The possibility of someone barreling into it didn't even cross my mind. I was completely still for a long time, not thinking, and it was hard to tell how many minutes had passed before my brain began working again.

I knew I had to do something, because the longer I waited, the more chances I took with the car just sitting there. I weighed whether it would be crazier to keep going toward the foggy, unclear destination of "elsewhere," or to simply turn around. I concluded that I no longer felt the hunger to run away that had been consuming me. But the thought of going back almost made me sick . . .

I looked to the mountains for answers, but they stood still and silent, guarding their secrets. It would've been easier if I'd died, I thought, but then realized I didn't exactly want to die. Not anymore. The cold indifference I'd felt just a few hours earlier had abated. I missed my family. I guess I cared about them after all. And even though I tried, I couldn't stop the tears from rolling down my cheeks.

I cried for a long time. Too long, probably. And when I'd stopped crying, I saw that the sky was no longer black, and that the signs of early dawn were creeping in all around. A bird sang a happy melody. The stars, one by one, began to disappear, and I knew it wouldn't be long before the world woke up and found me here.

Best to be found on my own terms, I decided.

So I wandered back to the car, and I carefully turned it around. Luckily, the road was just wide enough, and I headed back home.

I didn't bother speeding. I didn't bother to think what might happen when I got back. That was a problem for later. In any event, I'd committed worse crimes. I wondered if my parents had even noticed I was gone.

I looked at the clock. 5:53 a.m. Not likely, as only a crazy person would be up this early. And they were trying their best to be normal people now.

Carried along by the meandering road, I passed a few other cars. It was bright enough, I realized, that I no longer needed headlights to light the way. Gradually, the sun's orange glow seeped down from the jagged peaks, burning away the shadows as it went.

I noticed many things that had been invisible to me only hours before. To my left, for example, a waterfall cascaded serenely over the rocky slopes. On the right, a field of flowers sprawled across the grassy incline. Faint memories of having once hiked in these mountains tugged at the back of my mind.

I soon passed a lone tree that seemed to be barely clinging to life. Somehow, it had made a home in the cold, nearly vertical stone cliffs. As I passed the tree, the road began to descend, and my foot left the gas, and I coasted back towards the jaws of civilization. There would be time to think later. For now, my head was empty as I watched the great rocky monoliths recede in my rear-view mirror.

The town was just waking up. While I may have been driving right past the houses, they didn't seem real. I looked around and wondered who would be crazy enough to live in a tiny town like this in the middle of nowhere. A few minutes later, I pulled off the highway and plunged into the maze of narrow streets that made up the town, and before I knew it, I reached East Oakwood Street.

Six blocks to go.

I could turn around right now.

Five blocks to go.

What will they say? They must be awake by now.

Four blocks to go.

What can they say? It's just another crime to them.

Three blocks.

Why should I miss people who never gave a crap about me?

Two blocks.

God, I miss you Becky. Why'd you have to get yourself killed?

One block.

Too late to turn back, I guess.

Before I pulled into the driveway, I had one final thought, about leaving again. I wasn't quite crazy enough to do it, I guess, because I was turning the wheel before the idea even left my mind.

I glanced around. It was hard to tell if the lights were on. The curtains always made it hard to tell. It was an old house, bruised and battered, but old houses come cheap, and that was why we lived here. Before I'd even pulled the car to a stop, I saw the door crack open.

Dammit. I stayed in the car for a moment, considering whether to stay in the car for a moment more. And I did. And I almost stayed for another moment, but there was Dad in the doorway, and he might've been annoyed, or mad, or angry, or livid, but it was hard to tell. So I turned the key and opened the car door, and I thought about how it wasn't damaged, thank god, and that all I'd really done was take a little joyride. He didn't have to know how far I'd gone, or where, or that I'd nearly died.

And then we were face to face, and I was terrified, until I felt his arms close around me.

I just stood there, numbly, as he hugged me closer. Though I fought to push them back, I couldn't stop the tears from breaking free. Reluctantly, I let the tension melt away. I fell forward, wrapping my arms around him.

Somehow, in that moment, things were perfect. But the moment ended too soon. As we stepped apart, I gazed into his eyes. There was certainly a hint of frustration behind them, but they were overwhelmingly filled with concern.

"Papa, I . . ." My sentence trailed off as I searched for something to say.

"Just don't let it happen again, Chiquita."

"I won't, Papa. I promise," I said, handing him the keys.

"Now your ma ain't awake yet, so . . . Here, let's sit for a minute."

He took a seat on the wooden steps of our porch. I joined him, and for a while, neither of us spoke. He reached into his pocket and pulled out a pack of cigarettes. His hands were shaking as he lit up. After taking a puff, he finally looked at me.

"Look, Chiquita, I get what you're going through. I remember when I'd just gotten out of high school, I had this buddy, Zach. He and I were tight like glue, you know? Said we'd die for each other." He took another drag, and we both looked toward the horizon as the smoke hovered around us. "So it was tough, you know, when he decided to kill himself."

I felt a hot rush of anger. "You think Becky –"

"Shh. I never said that."

"She would never! You don't know her."

"Sarah, please. I'm not trying to tell you what was going through her head that night. You're right, I didn't know her like you. Look, I'm just saying . . . I've lost a friend before. A friend I thought I would never lose. I know what you're going through."

"No you don't," I said, my anger getting the better of me. It was funny how easily I fell back into old habits. "You don't get it at all. Becky was everything I had!"

My dad sighed softly. "I don't wanna do this again, Sarah."

"Oh yeah? Well, you didn't seem to care yesterday. Or the day before that."

I jumped to my feet. He just sat there, saying nothing, which only angered me more.

"You never cared if you yelled at me before, so why start caring now? You could've cared before Becky went out and got herself killed, and then maybe we wouldn't be here!"

Still, the idiot didn't say a word. I looked back at the car, wondering how I could've been crazy enough to come back here. I thought of running away again, but my heart wasn't in it. And I knew deep down that this anger wasn't right. As I stood there, breathing in the scent of fresh tobacco, a million hate-filled words entered and exited my mind, but the burning rage began to cool.

My dad looked down, rubbing the bridge of his nose. I noticed the bags under his eyes. I was hit with a pang of regret. I sat back down next to him, staring at the ground in front of us, fiddling with my hands.

"Sorry," I managed. He just looked at me, a hint of a smile on his face.

Suddenly, the door creaked open behind us. I turned to see Mom standing in the doorway. Her messy blonde hair and her robe made it clear that she hadn't been up long.

"What are you two doing out so early?" she asked. I began to panic as I imagined her discovering what I'd done. Dad may have let it go, but Mom was different. Just as I was about to open my mouth, Dad cleared his throat.

Shit, I'm done for.

"We went for an early drive," he said with a grin, jingling the car keys.

"At this hour of the morning? You're crazy," she said, shaking her head. "Well, I'm glad you two are getting along." There was a pause, and then, "I know it's been hard, Sarah. Just remember, we're here for you."

"I know, Ma."

"Why don't I make some pancakes? It's not much, but I know they're your favorite."

"Thanks, Ma. That'd be great."

As she disappeared inside, we stood up to follow her, but Dad stopped.

"Look," he said, "I don't know when you left, or how far you went, or what you saw out there, but I'm glad you decided to come back. And I know how it feels, and I know you're hurting, and I know we're not there enough for you. And I know it shouldn't have taken the death of your best friend and you running away for me to realize that, and I'm sorry. And I know I don't say it enough, but I love you, Sarah. And I know words don't mean much, so I'll try to show you more often."

I was crying again. Stupid feelings. But then he wrapped his arms around me, and again I melted into him, and all the problems in the world didn't matter for those quiet moments.

"Alright, now how 'bout we get some pancakes?" he said.

And with that, we went inside.

Shawn McAllister is a senior at Montezuma-Cortez High School. He loves expressing myself through writing, and is excited for the chance to share his work with a wider audience.

Seasons in the Sun

Katayoun Medhat

Legs dangling in water,
a woman
caresses her pregnant belly
as if it is
the head of a child.

Fearless in trust
sturdy-legged toddlers
launch themselves into open arms,
shrieking with joy.

For them
each year brings gains,
or should:
The rejection of float aids.
The spurning of a waiting embrace.

Solo crossing the width of the pool!
Conquering the slide!
Braving the diving board!

In just a few years
they'll jostle, and race,
and chase,
and vault headfirst,
into water,
and holler,
and splash
and whoop,
wrestle,
and dunk,
until the lifeguard's shrill whistle trills.

The toddlers I once observed
dog-paddling in swim vests
may now be these lifeguards,
watching over me
as I swim,
 lap after lap,
my stiffening limbs
resisting speed.

Cocooned in
youth's golden armor.
they know
they'll never be as old,
nor as slow
 as this.

From me each year
takes away a length or two.
But not the joy.
The sheer joy of moving
through clear cool water
under the blue, blue sky
seared by the sun.

The water's lapping
muffles the cackling of crows
perching on branches
that sway high up
over this blessed oasis
in the valley's parched lap.

Katayoun Medhat is the author of The Milagro Mysteries, *featuring unlikely cop Franz Kafka. She lives in the UK and likes to spend her summers in the Four Corners, where she is grateful, every day, for Cortez's wonderful outdoor pool. You can find her at www.katayounmedhat.com.*

Learning How to Be a
Good Ancestor

Amorina Lee-Martinez

I grew up in the Mancos Valley, Colorado, with mountains to the north and east, desert to the west, and the Ute Mountain Ute Reservation land to the south. Just down the road from where I grew up lived a Mormon family. They had a daughter who was the same age as me and we played together outside often, returning home in need of a bath regularly. My friend would say, "God made dirt and dirt don't hurt," and I agreed. Even though we would get dirty playing outside, I never felt dirty. I felt like we were adventuring in an unspoiled land.

When I moved to Boulder for school, I felt the difference in the land. The dense, concrete, litter-ridden world of urban blight had been a distant concept to me as a child in rural Colorado. The much larger and faster growing population of the Front Range felt like a flood of intensity. While in the Environmental Studies program at CU, I came to think of Western migration as a tide that hasn't stopped rising since the first trappers and goldrushes brought waves of newcomers in the 1700s and 1800s. The Rocky Mountains are like a seawall. The swells of people coming West splashed up against those high peaks and crashed backward into themselves settling at the foot of the peaks. Now Denver and the whole Front Range is filling up with the sea of folks moving in. Some early Euro-American citizens trickled further into the mountains to trap beaver for high dollar furs, mine for precious ores, or to uphold the pastoral way of life promoted by the Jeffersonian ideal and the Homestead Act. Today whole streams of people follow in those first strenuous footsteps to travel west of the Front Range and settle. After I finished school in Boulder, I followed that westward flow back to Montezuma County to live in Cortez in lands that appear far from the fray.

I used to think the problem was too many people when I went outside to visit places along the Front Range. I would reminisce about my little hometown where I grew up and miss that sparsely populated, pristine land and the dark star-studded skies. Until I began to pursue my college studies, I did not know how ignorant I was about the concept of "pristine" versus "not pristine". When I first thought and used the term "pristine" about my environment in rural southwest Colorado, I was making some assumptions. First, I assumed that people and landscapes in rural regions encountered little to no negative consequences from the mass migration West compared to the Front Range. Second, I assumed that I could see, smell or taste any negative impacts from humans. Third, I assumed that my way of life was not having any negative impacts on other people or the surrounding environment. I have begun to deepen my knowing about the history of my homeland in Colorado which renders some of my previous assumptions obsolete.

First, rural regions have not been safe from the negative consequences of Westward migration. I have learned how the U.S. government aided Westward expansion by making it legal to encroach upon Indigenous people who roamed in this region in order for newcomers to appropriate land. Bands of Ute people used to thrive living nomadically all over the territory that is Colorado and the Four Corners today. They were relegated into reservations in Utah and into a small strip in the southwest corner of Colorado by government force and violence. The Diné people, after having reservation borders imposed upon them in Utah, Arizona and New Mexico, were further forced into accepting mining and power production on their land, receiving all of the pollution and few of the benefits brought by these industries (Thompson 2018; Decker 2004; "Early History" 2022).

Second, while some pollution has been quite visible to me, other pollutants are hidden in plain sight. Once Native peoples were extracted from the land, the Euro-American newcomers could extract what they wanted from the land. Where I grew up, some of these industrial activities include nearby coal power plants on the Navajo Reservation like Four Corners Power Plant in New Mexico and the now defunct Navajo Generating Station near Page, Arizona. These plants have caused mercury pollution in the Four Corners region to be at the highest levels in the nation (Thompson 2018). I learned about acid mine drainage all over the Rockies, which is mostly invisible. But, the bright yellow Gold King Mine spill on the Animas River in 2015 was a stark example that harmed the river ecosystem and people far downstream. I also became aware of historic uranium mining in Western Colorado, radioactive waste contamination at the White Mesa Uranium Mill in Utah, and plutonium processing at Rocky Flats on the Front Range. All these operations have caused environmental and public health issues but have been swept under the rug by corporate and government interests alike (Thompson 2018; Decker 2004; "Early History" 2022; Iverson 2013; Grand Canyon Trust 2024).

Third, my way of life does have negative impacts on people and the environment. I now understand the land in which I grew up and played is not rightfully owned by anyone currently living on it. A white family had homesteaded what is now my family's property in Mancos in the late 1800s against the wishes of the local Ute people (Freeman 1958). Christian and Mormon religious worldviews suppressed the Indigenous worldviews. The statement my friend made that "God made dirt," holds a deeper message that it was her God, a deity of the European Americans who made dirt, and for whom? And, where does that leave the Ute, who lived on the dirt for time immemorial?

These legacies of genocide and polluting operations were once invisible to me. I was able to be ignorant to the human harm and widespread pollution that still impacts this land and people. It had never occurred to me that I might be a culprit. But I benefit from historical colonialism and I need electricity and fossil fuels and high-tech equipment. The device on which I type this story requires heavy metals like lead and mercury made available by extractive mining. Indigenous homeland appropriation, power generation and mining make our American ways of life possible in the West, while simultaneously harming Indigenous ways of life.

I no longer feel clean in the dirt. I get to live in beautiful landscapes, but someone else used to freely live here. Someone else is working in a mine or is exposed to devastating levels of radiation for the purpose of economy, of war, of keeping our lifestyles abundant. And I have likely been exposed to residual contamination spreading from intensive extraction and processing centers, like the former Rocky Flats facilities on the Front Range, derelict hard rock mines in the Rockies, and White Mesa Uranium Mill just over the border in Utah.

Now I understand that to live in the West is to live in a land that carries the legacy of human and environmental impact. We must look at this legacy and face it directly. The Ute and Diné people, among hundreds of other tribes across the nation, carried ancestral knowledge about how to sustain themselves and the land. White newcomers disregarded and worked to erase this knowledge and responsibility, and intentionally extracted from the land for wealth and power at the expense of non-White cultures and lands and without considering people in the future—the people who currently live here.

A man from my hometown named Ira Freeman wrote a history of the southwest Colorado region in 1958. His entries about the Utes provide an example of how White people disregarded Indigenous ways of life. He wrote: "He (the Ute Indian) lived in one room where he cooked, ate and slept, and he lived with vermin and under conditions that were far from clean or sanitary." Freeman assumed that Ute people – who have lived in tune with the landscape in Colorado and the Four Corners far longer than any Europeans – lived unsatisfactory lives, and argues that if they lived like him, aspired to be like White people, their lives would be better. In fact, when the US government pushed the Ute Mountain Ute Tribe onto their current reservation in the corner of Colorado, they were forced to live without access to consistent good quality water sources for over 100 years.

With regard to how Ute livelihoods were changed by U.S. government regulation and reservations, Freeman wrote: "The new life the Ute Indian has today is already infinitely better than the old way. Yet he resisted the change. It could not have been expected that he would understand. The Ute Indian is still a primitive person in a way..." From this perspective, colonialism was necessary and the Indigenous people who resisted didn't know any better (Freeman 1958). This rhetoric is one source, and example, of the ideology which mandated that damage be done to Indigenous people, by forcing them to live according to puritanical belief.

Beginning in the late 1800s, some of my White ancestors from Nebraska and Kansas left a legacy of extraction and pollution, which are still present today, with little or no responsibility for the long-term effects on people or the land. When it comes to landscape-level change, we are all downstream, affected by the actions of other people. Importantly, Indigenous people more often feel the negative consequences of environmental impacts. We not only need to take into account people who live downstream physically, but who live downstream temporally.

How can I be a better ancestor than my White ancestors were to me? Before they were kicked out, fenced in, or forced to assimilate, my Indigenous ancestors from the Sonoran Desert had lived in this landscape for countless generations without leaving persistent pollutants behind. The difference in behavior between my White ancestors and my Indigenous ancestors was their understanding of, relationship with, and responsibility to this land, presently called America. I think the best way to live in the West today is to take responsibility for how our wellbeing is connected to the landscape, whether subsisting, mining, farming, ranching, operating large industry, recreating, or moving in. We must take care of the land in the same way that it takes care of us. That is our responsibility to future generations.

Knowing this history makes it clear to me that "pristine" is the wrong characterization of my home valley. The White society around me where I grew up has been avoiding our past of human and environmental harm. With so much destruction, perhaps it is easier to hide the past than to learn from it. It has been hard for me to learn these truths about my homeland, being half Indigenous and half White. My mother is Native American and grew up in Los Angeles displaced from her ancestral homeland in the Sonoran Desert. Her generation had to choose between assimilation and poverty. She negotiated living the impacts of language and cultural colonialism by learning how to read and was able to find solace in books. Through her self-determination and help from allies, she became highly educated and today she advocates for Native American educational self-determination. She married my father who is a White man from Kansas, and my brother and I are the paradoxical and multicultural result.

My seemingly conflicting heritage helps me to see both sides of Westward expansion – the colonizers and the colonized. Yet I find little comfort in being of both worlds because I don't feel like I fully belong in either. Perhaps this means I can be part of creating a whole new world that incorporates both. Indigenous perseverance over centuries provides insight about what it means to maintain ways of life and to create new worlds. Tribes have been working to turn back destruction from colonialism for over five centuries and have been adapting to climate change for longer (Estes 2019; Flatow 2020). The Indigenous people of America are not giving up. Nick Estes of the Lower Brule Sioux Tribe said in an interview that solutions for our future lie in kinship we share with the land we occupy as Natives and non-Natives. Indigenous struggles have always been tied to land that was taken. To be indigenous is to "make kin" – to relate to the land and to fellow humans and non-humans as familiars. To be kin is to treat all earthly beings with respect as relatives in a reciprocal relationship. If it is possible for colonizers to relate with the colonized as kin and as knowledgeable caretakers of the land, then it may be possible to create a new world where the land and all people are equals. If people and land can be kin, then perhaps people and land can be cared for as such for generations to come (Estes 2019).

Though the history of Westward expansion can be painful to understand, I choose to learn about this past and to learn *from* it because it affects our current lives. I feel so inspired by the continued resistance of Indigenous people to live, rebuild, and maintain their cultural heritages and kinship with ancestral lands, despite many persistent forms of colonial harm. I want to care for my homeland

and create history that people do not want to hide. I want posterity to be grateful for my actions. As a citizen of the Yampa River Valley in northwest Colorado once said, "Good planners make good ancestors (Williams 2001)." To me this means that how we take care of fellow people and landscapes today will directly affect people and landscapes tomorrow. For the people who will be alive long after I am dead, I want to be a responsible ancestor who will leave my world better than how I found it. I begin by learning the story of our past so that I can create a better story for our future.

Amorina Lee-Martinez was born and raised in Mancos, Colorado on ancestral Ute Mountain Ute lands and now lives and works in Montezuma County. She comes from Afro-Cuban, Indigenous Mexican and European heritage. She completed her PhD in Environmental Studies at CU Boulder in 2022 researching the historical context of present-day Dolores River land and water management.

References

Decker, Peter R. 2004. *"The Utes Must Go!": American Expansion and the Removal of a People*. Golden, Colorado: Fulcrum Publishing.

"Early History." 2022. Southern Ute Indian Tribe History. 2022. https://www.southernute-nsn.gov/history/.

Flatow, Ira. n.d. "How Native American Communities Are Addressing Climate Change." Science Friday. Accessed February 7, 2020. https://www.sciencefriday.com/segments/native-american-communities-climate-change/.

Freeman, Ira S. 1958. *A History of Montezuma County Colorado: Land of Promise and Fulfillment*. Boulder, CO: Johnson Publishing Company.

Grand Canyon Trust. 2024. "White Mesa Uranium Mill." Grand Canyon Trust. 2024. https://www.grandcanyontrust.org/white-mesa-uranium-mill.

"Indigenous People's Resistance--Interview with Nick Estes." 2019.

RISE UP Alternative Radio. University of Colorado, Denver.

Iverson, Kristen. 2013. *Full Body Burden: Growing Up in the Nuclear Shadow of Rocky Flats*. New York, NY: Broadway Paperbacks.

Thompson, Johnathan P. 2018. *River of Lost Souls: The Science, Politics, and Greed Behind the Gold King Mine Disaster*. Salt Lake City, UT: Torrey House Press.

Williams, Florence. 2001. "Colorado's Yampa Valley: Planning for Open Space." In *Across the Great Divide: Explorations in Collaborative Conservation and the American West*. Washington DC: Island Press.

About the Editors

Chuck Greaves, the author of seven novels, has been a finalist for many of the top honors in crime fiction including the Shamus, Lefty, Macavity, and Audie Awards, as well as the New Mexico-Arizona, Oklahoma, and Colorado Book Awards and the Harper Lee Prize for Legal Fiction. His 2012 novel *Hard Twisted* (Bloomsbury) was hailed by the Los Angeles Times as "a gritty, gripping read, and one that begs to be put on film" while his 2015 novel *Tom & Lucky* (Bloomsbury) was a *Wall Street Journal* "Ten Best Mysteries of 2015" selection. His latest novel *The Chimera Club*, the fourth installment in his critically acclaimed Jack MacTaggart series of legal mysteries (Minotaur), was a 2023 Colorado Book Award finalist and was named the "Best Mystery Novel of 2022" by the Colorado Authors League. You can visit him at www.chuckgreaves.com.

Lisa C. Taylor holds an MFA in Creative Writing from Stonecoast/University of Southern Maine. She has three published collections of poetry, two published collections of short stories, and her forthcoming novel, *The Shape of What Remains* will be published in March 2025. Lisa's honors include the Elizabeth Shanley Gerson

Lecture in Irish Literature with Irish writer Geraldine Mills, a Surdna Arts Fellowship that enabled her to spend a summer in Ireland, a Hugo House New Works Fiction Award, Pushcart nominations in fiction and poetry, and Best-of-the-Net nominations in fiction and poetry. She's received writing residencies from the Tyrone Guthrie Centre in Ireland, Vermont Studio Center, and Willowtail Springs in Colorado. Her work has appeared in anthologies and numerous literary journals. Lisa formerly taught creative writing at a university and an arts magnet high school. She currently teaches online, presents at writing conferences nationwide, and co-directs the Mesa Verde Writers Conference with writer Mark Stevens.

The son of two librarians, **Mark Stevens** was raised in Lincoln, Massachusetts and has worked as a reporter, television news producer, and in public relations. He's the author of *The Fireballer* (2023, Lake Union), named Best Baseball Novel by *Twin Bill* literary magazine and named a Best Baseball Book of the Year by *Spitball Magazine*. Thomas & Mercer will publish *No Lie Lasts Forever* in April of 2025, the first of a new series. Stevens is also the author of The Allison Coil Mystery Series including *Antler Dust, Buried by the Roan, Trapline, Lake of Fire,* and *The Melancholy Howl*. *Buried by the Roan, Trapline,* and *Lake of Fire* were all finalists for the Colorado Book Award (2012, 2015 and 2016 respectively). *Trapline* won. Stevens has had short stories published in *Ellery Queen Mystery Magazine, Denver Noir* (2022, Akashic Books), and *Crimes Against Nature* (2024, Down & Out Books). In 2016 and again in 2023, Stevens was named Rocky Mountain Fiction Writers' Writer of the Year. Stevens hosts a regular podcast for Rocky Mountain Fiction Writers and has served as president of the Rocky Mountain Chapter for Mystery Writers of America.